The House Breaker

WALKER WALLACE

inter alia press
USA

ISBN: 0692578226
ISBN-13: 9780692578223

DEDICATION

For Father Escalante

CONTENTS

ACKNOWLEDGMENTS

I want to thank Scott Fitzgerald, Ernest Hemingway, Willa Cather, Cormac McCarthy, Wallace Stegner, A.B. Guthrie, Jr., Marilynne Robinson, Ivan Doig, Kurt Vonnegut, Walker Percy, Sinclair Lewis, and Flannery O'Connor for filling my mind with ideas.

PROLOGUE

I went back to Ohio
But my pretty countryside
Had been paved down the middle
By a government that had no pride

The Pretenders

It was all I had. It really was. My savings account was reset to zero. My checking account. Zero. I'd shaved some off the retirement. I'd closed my investments. Sold all the bonds. Broken my rule against borrowing: $4500 on my home equity line.

I went over to the bank for the cashier's check. They had it ready for me. I signed for it. Looked at the numbers. $85,254.27. I put it in my pocket and went out to the truck.

I drove to Main Street and out of town. The speed limit picked up from thirty to forty. I immediately had a tailgater. The speed limit went to fifty. The tailgater got closer. I have an old truck. It takes a minute or two to get up to speed. Most drivers don't have a minute. Let alone two. The highway straightened. I heard the turbo open. I saw the black cloud of diesel exhaust in my mirror. The tailgater boomed past. Seventy miles an hour. I looked down. I was up to fifty-two. I held steady. Instantly I had another tailgater. Several. I was at the front of the train. No one wanted to pass so I lead the whole pack across the valley to the freeway exit. I try not to be too aggressive. But sometimes I think about buying one of those bumper stickers: *The closer you get, the slower I go.* I drove up the southbound ramp leading five or six anxious motorists. I put my foot to the floor and worked up through fifty towards sixty. It wasn't enough. As soon as the

1

travel lane came into sight the tailgaters blasted across the apron trying to pass me. Trying to pass each other. Trying to pass the big rigs that were already in the lane. I merged and got up to around seventy. I settled down. All my friends had disappeared.

I quickly made new ones. I was in the way. I was in people's way. They were in a hurry. Headed south. Headed for Vegas, for San Bernardino, for Phoenix. I don't know. Headed for San Diego. For the ocean. For Disney World. I don't know. Maybe it was just a rush to Costco. To Cabelas. It was Thursday afternoon. Business hours. Non-holiday business hours. Campers. Boats. Mountain bikes. Audis. Escalades. Toyotas of every description. Hondas. Tinted glass. Flashing past. Ain't nobody got to work anymore. The freeway is crowed all the time. I should probably stay off of it. Use the old highway. My truck can approximate the speed limit. But that makes me fifteen miles per hour slower than everyone else. I'm a hazard. I'm in the way.

I approached town. The city. I came into the sprawl. Plastic housing crawling across the hillsides. The traffic was worse. I thought of Lyman Ward. *The apple trees are in blossom, and I thought for a while I was hearing the traffic from the freeway that has split and ruined this town, but when I listened carefully it was the sound of thousands of bees up to their thighs in pollen.* I took the second exit and turned east towards the mountains. The main boulevard. Six lanes wide. I eased through four or five lights. I turned left into a small parking lot. Southwest Title Company.

The man with whom I'd made an appointment wasn't in the office. His secretary met me. Pretty. Buxom. She rushed to apologize.

—Russ was called away. He had an important closing across town. He said that you would be bringing cash. He said there wouldn't be much for you to sign.

—OK.

—He said that I could do it. He said that I could do it with you. I mean. He said that I could handle it. The closing I mean. If that is OK with you.

—I guess so.

—Great. Please. Will you come in here?

She lead me into a tacky board room. Dark. Heavy drapes. Cheap furniture. Florescent lights. There was a small portfolio on the table. She crossed to the other side and pushed it over to me. It had sticky notes. *Sign Here.* There were four or five of them. She leaned over to explain it. I could see down her shirt. Was she doing that on purpose? *He said that I could do it with you? Said that I could handle it?* I looked at her left hand. No ring.

Please. Sit.

I sat.

—Here.

She took a pen from her pocket and slipped it across the table. I opened the portfolio and went through it. I agreed to the deed. I agreed to the insurance. I agreed to the amount. When I was done with the signing I leaned back and reached into my pocket. I pulled out the cashier's check. I signed it and put it on the portfolio. I spun the portfolio and slid it across the table to her. I looked at her again. She met my eye.

—Terrific. Let me make copies and put together a packet for you to take.

She rushed out. I watched her go. I leaned back and stared at the wall. I started to feel pretty good. It was done. It was expensive. But it was done. I sat there for eight or ten minutes. I looked at my watch. It was almost five. The work day was over. Time to celebrate. With her? With the secretary?

It was stupid. I'm not really like that. I mean. I don't go around picking up girls. I'm not good at it for one thing. And it is stupid. It really is.

—Here you go Mr. Smith. I apologize for the delay.

—Well thanks for helping me with this. I'm sorry to come here so late in the day. You must be ready to close the office.

—Oh. No. No problem.

—Let me make it up to you. Buy you a sandwich. A drink. You name it. We could go over to Zee's.

—Really. It's no big deal. If my desk weren't such a wasteland I could have made sure all your documents were ready sooner.

—You're the T.S. Eliot of receptionists huh?

Brilliant. It was brilliant. It really was. If that didn't impress her what would. I mean. I stun myself with my brilliance sometimes. Where does it come from? This high-brow twentieth century repartee? I amaze myself. Myself. I amaze myself. But that is evidently as far as it goes.

She smiled. She looked blank. There was a beat. A second beat. It didn't seem like she was impressed. It didn't even seem like she was sentient. Her phone buzzed. Saved by the bell. She picked it up.

—Hey. Yeah. I know. But he won't eat olives. You know that. Get the other. OK. I'm with a customer. OK. Bye.

She hung up. Looked up. Gave me another smile.

—My boyfriend. He can't seem to remember that my son doesn't like olives on his pizza.

The traffic was worse than ever. I decided to go to the big liquor store on the other side of town. I could hardly afford it but I thought they might have some good wine on sale. I stayed in the right lane and patiently stopped at all the lights. Important people zoomed around me. I took a left at the end of Center Street and went down past the Home Depot. I parked.

The store was busy. I skipped the beer. Skipped the hard stuff. Went to the wines. The reds. Chilean Malbec. Californian Cabernet. Australian Shiraz. There was a pretty good bottle of shiraz for under ten. It was going on the credit card. I took it to the counter. There was a guy in front of me. Dozens of bottles. Everything. Liquor. Wine. Beer. Mixers. Chasers. Condiments. He was loud. Gregarious.

—Got paid today.

—Oh yeah.

The checker was hip to it: A thirty something dude with a bunch of hair under his lip.

—I'm blowing it all.

—I guess you are.

—Yeah. Supporting the economy. Doing my part.

They evidently knew each other. The guy was a regular.

—Having some people over. You should stop by.

—Cool. Save me some of that Fireball.

—Fuck. Dude.

The guy slid his two boxes off the counter and went out. I was next. I went forward with one bottle of wine. On sale. I looked at the checker. He looked past me. He slid my card.

—Want your receipt?

—Please.

I took my bottle and the little slip of paper. I went out to the truck. I left the parking lot and idled up to the light. Green. Onto the northbound ramp. Foot on the floor. Behind me a Mercedes. Around me on the apron. *Get out of my way you hayseed. Can't you see this is a Mercedes.* I worked my way into the line-up of trucks in the slow lane.

I parked in front of a ramshackle former farm house. I took my papers and my bottle of wine across the yard. My yard. My house. I looked it over. With pleasure. Nice old graceful hand-built lines. A sag here and some fading paint there. But neat. Clean. Solid. Built of native materials. Built to stay. Shaded now by a couple of elms.

I went into the kitchen and opened the wine. I poured a small glass and took it to the porch. I sat there for a moment with the sun getting low and a dove in mourning. Just one moment. Then a truck turned up the street. A big diesel. The driver floored it. Forty MPH in under three seconds. It roared. Seeing me the driver braked hard and skidded to the shoulder in a cloud of dust. It was a neighbor. He lived a couple of blocks over. On the town council. Or county commission. Or something. Glenn. Left the truck running. Loud. Rattle rattle tap tap. Came across the yard.

—Wanted to talk to you about something.

—Yeah.

—Saw you sitting out here.

—Uh-huh.

—Going to be a vote.

—Oh.

—University wants to build a medical center.

—Really?

—Yeah. Now. Ya understand. This will be great for the whole area. Important for the community. Put us on the map. You know. Biggest thing between—Hell—Boise and San Berdew.

—Oh.

—The best site for it is a little south of the current athletic center. Unfortunately a few of those people down there don't want to sell. They're holding us up. Know what I mean? The thing is. I think we should just force 'em out. Right of emigrant dominion or some such thing our attorney tells me. But the rest of 'em want to have a vote. See? Have the community vote. You know?

—Uh-huh.

—Great thing for the county. Lots of jobs. The kind of thing we really need. I know you ain't got kids. But you will have. And let me tell you. You'll want to provide opportunities for them kids. Take my two sons now. Would really like to have them stay in the area. But the jobs are few and far between. Know what I mean? The really good jobs. The jobs to buy a house and raise a family on. We need jobs for our kids.

His two sons were a couple of hefty over-fed bovines. Early twenties. Covered in tattoos. High-school diplomas. Semi-literate at best. Lazy. Slack-jawed. Swaggering. They were unemployed. They sure were. But who would hire them? Captain Glanton? The Russian Mafia? That pair didn't need an opportunity at an American medical center; they needed an opportunity at a gulag on the banks of the Lena.

I looked out at the street. The dusk was growing. Glenn's truck was juddering. The door ajar. He was still talking. I realized I was hungry. Time to go in for a sandwich. Or at least some bread with a slab of butter.

—So you see we need this. And it's not just me. All your neighbors. Look at Jack over there. His boy. Out of work. Our county needs an opportunity like this. A big break. A boost. A real shot in the arm.

Shot in the arm? I thought of Pappy O'Daniel. I looked at Glenn.

—Well. OK.

—I knew we could count on your vote.

I stood up. I reached for my empty glass. I turned toward the door.

—Well. I bess be on my way. Good to talk with you. Don't forget to be neighborly. Stop in any time.

—Thanks. Talk to you later.

I went in the house while Glenn scurried to the truck. I heard the door slam. I heard the wheels turn. I heard the engine roar. I heard the brakes squeal at the stop sign. I heard the engine roar down the other block. I got the bread knife and a loaf of rye. It was quiet in the kitchen.

1

The first thing I did after the deed recorded was remove the satellite dish. I went over there with my pick-up and a ladder. I propped the ladder against the facia and climbed it carrying my cordless drill. After unplugging the cable I used the drill to remove the mounting screws. I didn't brace the dish. I let it fall. It thumped on the ground. I climbed down and threw the whole thing into the bed of the pick-up.

I walked along the back of the house. There was a broken basketball backstop with a bent rim. It was attached to a steel pipe. The pipe was cemented into the patio. I went back to the truck. I rummaged for the hacksaw. Bracing my shoulder against the pipe I cut through the base. It was hard work. I was winded by the time the whole thing toppled. I picked it up by the pipe and dragged it to the front. I threw it on the truck.

I looked into the carport. It was full of trash. Broken furniture. Computer printers. Dirty furnace filters. I found a crumpled bicycle. I threw the bike on the truck. Along with an old lawn mower that had obviously been run over—wheels askew.

In the house I found an abandoned sink fixture on the floor of the bathroom. There was trash everywhere. Not just cheap junk left behind when they moved out but actual trash. Spoiled food and soiled diapers. I found a Daisy BB-gun without a stock. Along with the sink fixture it went into the pile in the back of the pick-up.

After an hour I had a jumble of metal and plastic refuse in the back of the truck. It was mostly steel. It was a tangled mess. The detritus of lives lived without care—just go ahead and break it and leave it there. I drove to the recycler. His name is Roberts. He pays $50 per ton for "iron." We sorted the tangled mess. Along with all the plastic I had 200 pounds of iron. Roberts gave me five dollars.

I'm a house breaker. I break houses. My name is John Smith. I live in the western United States—in Box Elder County. John Smith is a common name in the western United States. It is probably one of those names that is at the top of the list for common names. Breaking houses is not a common occupation.

Breaking houses isn't really a job. I don't receive a pay packet for doing it. I pay to break houses. Broken houses don't pay me. For that there is Illium. The book publisher. I edit books. Illium pays me for that. I take home about $4000 per month. I'm a "senior" editor. I live on half of my pay. The rest goes into the business. The house breaking business.

I've been breaking houses for about six years. This is my second one. The first is about a block and a half from where I live. It is now a .35 acre vacant lot. I grow pumpkins there. I sell the pumpkins in October for $.50 each. It is a self-serve business run from a wagon at the front of the lot. People usually pay. Most years I can make about $60 or $80 in pumpkin money by Halloween. In November the property taxes are due. They are currently $458.

My current project is next door to the house I live in. The people who used to own it were named Ewell. They were heavy-set. They dressed like gangsters from San Bernardino. The little boy was fat. He wore Oakland Raiders paraphernalia. The little girl was fat. She shat a lot. When the wind toppled the plastic trash bin filthy diapers spewed on the ground. The Ewells stepped over them on the way to the house from the truck.

I had to pass the front of the house when I walked to my pumpkin patch. Sometimes Ewell would be in the yard. There was a little dog. It shat a lot. Ewell watched it shit. He'd be wearing a cut-off T-shirt. He had a lot of tattoos. Usually he wanted to talk.

—What year is your Chevy?

— '89

—Run good?

—Yeah. I like it. Reliable.

—My wife's got that Dodge. Piece of shit. Our payment is $400 a month. We spend more than that every month fixing stuff. I told her to trade it in. Get one a them minivans or something. She won't. She likes the truck.

—What's it get for mileage?

—Oh shit. I don't know. It's horrible. Probably ten. Eleven.

The dog would sniff me. I hate dogs. I really do. I'd watch it closely. Ewell would call it. It would continue to sniff. Ewell would call loudly. The dog would ignore him. He'd get louder and louder as though the problem were a lack of volume. People are like that. They don't say things once. Quietly. They keep raising their voices. It's as though the universe will have a better understanding of their meaning if they can make a lot of noise. I hate noise. I really do.

For a while the Ewells had chickens. Remember the chicken era? Everybody had chickens. They were cute. They ate bugs. They laid eggs. The eggs were pure. They were local. Sometimes they were brown. Sometimes the chickens were too.

I don't know. I don't know what that was all about? The chicken era. It made me think of Willy Stark or something. Going out to the chicken farm. To keep up appearances. With the hens. They gave a nice homey atmosphere. They inspired confidence. Confidence. The chickens inspired confidence. Is that what it was for all those hipsters? They needed inspiration? And confidence? So they put some chickens in the yard.

Anyway. Ewell built a coop. I could see it across the fence in back. A real Gehry. Stacks of off kilter particle board strung with chicken wire. The chickens never spent a moment inside.

Ewell told me about it one day.

—My wife doesn't like to confine them.

—The chickens?

—Wants them to be free. You know.

—Yeah. Why'd you build the coop?

—I keep the feed in there.

Pretty soon the chickens made their way through the wire fence. I came home from work and found them in my yard. They'd trashed a flower bed. I picked them up and threw them—not gently—over the fence. I patched the hole in the fence. They found another. Another. Finally I built a new fence. Ewell stood and watched me.

The chicken feed attracted rats. The chickens attracted skunks. Raccoons. The particle board coop attracted yellow-jackets. It was a stinking mess. What? You mean owning farm animals has consequences? You mean you have to do something? The eggs don't simply cook themselves into my omelet?

Actually chickens attract more than skunks. I saw an article where the state wildlife people were saying that the chicken boom was accompanied by an urban coyote boom. Coyotes in the backyard. And foxes. Foxes! Surprise. Who ever heard of that? Yeah. The urban chicken craze. Shit momma we got a fox in the henhouse. But I digress.

After a while the chickens were gone—abandoned sickened flattened gone. But not the coop. Not the feed bin. Not the twisted wire. Just leave it. Why be forced to bend over? It is just more trash in the yard. Step over it on your way from the car to the house.

Not long after that the Ewells were gone too. I was a little surprised.

9

They moved out one weekend. They didn't say anything. I asked at the grocery store. Foreclosure. Foreclosure? They both had jobs. They were driving nice vehicles. It was not—I learned later—foreclosure. It was bankruptcy.

2

The distance between where I work and where I live is about eight miles. I commute sixteen miles per day. I leave my house each morning. Early. I drive through the neighborhood. Out onto Main Street. Down the State Highway.

I try to get to Illium by seven. I'm not usually the first one in the door. But the office is quiet at that time. I can get something done before the interruptions begin. I find that being an editor requires concentration. It can be difficult to concentrate at the office. There are meetings. Coffee breaks. Office parties. Birthdays.

I have a modular office—a cubical style office. The walls are thin and they don't reach the ceiling. But it does have a door. A door. I can close it. And sometimes I do. I put on my head-phones. Listen to something on the radio. Listen to Waylon; listen to Hozier. Not listening really but blocking the distractions.

I usually have lunch at the desk. A sandwich. Some water. People go out for lunch. Colleagues stop at the door. Ask me to join them. Once in a while I do. But not often. It's not that I don't like people; but mostly I don't really like people. The food is packed with fat and the conversation is packed with TV. Fucking TV.

By the middle of the afternoon I am running out of steam. It is hard to sit at the desk for eight or nine hours. I try to go by four-thirty. I follow the same route. Up the highway. Down Main Street. Through the neighborhood. I see the same things each day. Twice a day. Five days a week.

My first project was the Roundy house. I noticed it when Earl Roundy lived there. I noticed it because Earl was sitting by his garden each June morning when I drove by on the way to work at six-thirty or six-forty-five.

11

He was watering his carrots. His onions. His garden. One day I stopped to talk. Earl was sitting in an over-stretched lawn chair—when he moved it groaned.

—Morning.

—Morning.

—I'm John. I live on the next block.

—Uh-huh.

—Your garden looks great.

—Uh-huh. Where do you live?

—Over on the next block. Across from Billy Benson.

—Billy Benson's my cousin.

—Oh. Great.

—He's a sumbitch.

—Oh. Too bad.

The house was non-descript. Five years old. Covered in blue vinyl. (There must have been a sale on blue at the vinyl mine. Half the houses in the little development were blue.) But it was tidy. The garden was weeded. The grass was clipped. The ten-year old Buick on the slab was waxed. Earl didn't look young—or fit. But he kept his crap clean. His wife came out. Marlene.

—Morning.

—Morning.

—I stopped to admire your garden.

—You should see the onions we grew last year. The potatoes. We've still got some in the shed. Ate 'em all winter. Some left over. Would you like to see them?

—Sure.

—Here. Take some home.

A couple of years later Earl had a stroke. He went to a nursing home. Marlene said that she was moving out and that her grandson might move in. He did. With his girlfriend. And his dope. And his baggy stocking cap—winter spring summer fall. He didn't grow carrots in the side yard. Or onions. Potatoes. He didn't work at all. So far as I could tell. He certainly couldn't be bothered to pick up the empty Natural Light twelve-pack box—the cardboard suitcase—on the side walk. Shuffled from his car to the front door with his pants hanging so far off his ass that he had to reach down at the stoop to hold them on. I guess he was the shit. I mean it. That guy had it made.

After a while the FOR SALE sign came out. The house sat there looking a little run down. Finally a flipper bought it. Remember those? Take out a mortgage for a house you're not going to live in. Hold it for a year. Sell it for twice what you paid. Settle the mortgage. Walk away with the cash. Easy money. Everybody is doing it. Housewives are doing it. You'd be stupid not to do it. Can't lose.

I got the name for my vocation from an article I read in *The Economist*. It was about the ship breaking business in Bangladesh. Massive steel ships. Abandoned. Obsolete. Pulled up in the sand. These guys out there in shorts. Barefoot. Pulling a tanker apart by hand. Bare hands. It's bad say the NGOs. Dirty and dangerous. Bad. Bad for the environment. Bad for the barefoot barehanded worker. And it probably is. But there is something inspiring about it. At least to me. I'm going to pull apart your oil tanker with my hands. You consume shit and throw it on the ground. I pick it up and make something of it. I'm a ship breaker. I break ships.

I don't want to make too much of this. I break houses as a hobby. I break houses because I don't like trash. I break houses because I don't like seeing people living like pigs. In my neighborhood. (Actually I don't give a fuck how anybody lives. I just don't like noise and trash.) I break houses because I can. The ship breakers break because they must. They break to feed their families. They break to earn four dollars per day. They break to survive. This is life or death for them. There is nothing to do but do it. Me? I live in America. A country so filthy rich that most of us can sit on our asses and get fat. Let the chickens tear up the neighbor's garden. Shuffle over the trash on the sidewalk.

Anyway, the flipper of Roundy's house got lucky. He was able to move it. Here is how that worked: A young couple wanted to buy a house. Buy it quick. Buy it while there were houses available. Buy it before prices went up again. They went to the loan officer.

(What makes the seller of bad mortgages an "officer?" Can someone tell me that? An admiral is an officer; a colonel is an officer. Maybe I'm old fashioned but the word used to have a sound of hard-won authority—earned under live fire. Now the punk that pushes the deed across the table to me at the title company is an escrow officer. Everybody's a goddamn officer. I'm a fucking officer of broken houses. But I digress.)

They brought their pay stubs. The guy was a carpenter's helper. She was a teacher's aide. The loan officer looked at their data. He told them that they could afford a mortgage. They believed him. The figure he gave them was twice what they could afford. They still believed him. After all the interest rate was miniscule. By the time it escalated—by the time it adjusted—they would be able to return to the loan officer for a refinance job. "Streamlining" he called it. It sounded great. Streamlining makes everything better right? To paraphrase the Middle Brother: Their days were numbered but they were bad at math. In any case the mortgage was enough to buy the house. What a surprise.

They moved in that summer. They seemed alright. They weren't outdoor people. I never saw them in the yard. The first thing they bought was a dish. I guess they were TV people. Fucking TV. Anyway they didn't trash the place. They cut the grass. Made a few repairs. Built a fence in the backyard. They seemed OK.

Then the construction business slumped. To put it mildly. The Great Recession. The kid was out of work. I don't know what he did about it. It's tough. Honestly. I know what it is like. It's depressing. I've been there. Honest to God I have. You can't find a damn thing to do. You'd dig ditches if someone would give you a chance. Feed pigs. You'd sweat blood just to prove that you're no deadbeat. But day after day there is nothing. You get to the point—like Sturgill Simpson—you start to wondering which one of these banks you're gonna go rob. But you can't quit. You can't. You can't quit on your family.

Anyway. The wife got pregnant. Nine months later she still had her job. He was Mr. Mom. I rarely saw him. I rarely saw any of them. They quit cutting the grass. Quit picking up. Quit with the repairs. At some point they quit paying their bills. Quit. Quit. Quit. Pretty soon the work truck was gone. The crappy Dodge Neon was dragging its exhaust. A FOR SALE sign came out. The property was a mess. I stopped to look at the asking price. Insane. They were trying to get it all back. On a place that was never worth half of it. The price lasted two weeks. Then it was down by twenty grand. They streamlined it I guess. Two weeks later they were gone. The bank had evicted them.

3

On Sunday I went to church. It was one of those California come-as-you-are seeker-sensitive evangelical places. I should have known better. I sat off to the side in front of a well-dressed gray-haired couple. The row ahead of me was empty. The service started quietly with a decent hymn and some prayers. About ten minutes into it a guy and his wife shuffled into the empty row. It must have been Mr. Gold himself. The guy had weight-lifter's arms and legs. He had perfect hair. He even had a smooth fake-looking tan. I know all of this because he was dressed in the American uniform: sleeveless t-shirt shorts flip-flops.

Everywhere. All the time. Dead of winter. Stuck in a snow bank. Guy can't get out of the car because he is wearing shorts and flip-flops.

Five minutes later the couple was joined by their daughter and the daughter's boyfriend. The daughter looked like a porn star. I've never actually seen one but I've read about them. (How is it that one of my colleagues puts it? *I saw it on PBS.*) Mini-skirt thigh-high boots four-inch heels a pierced tongue. Boyfriend was tattoo boy. How could I tell?

Hey. It was a come-as-you-are kind of place. Feel free to express yourself. Go ahead. Piss in the pew.

Evidently mamma and daughter had little time to talk during the week so this was a good time to catch up. Boyfriend was texting. Pretty soon a phone rang. It was the guy behind me. He took the call.

—Yeah.

—They build aircraft parts.

—The county promised them a bunch of tax breaks if they would set-up a plant.

—Texas

—I'm working on a lease out at the airport.

—About two hundred thousand square feet.

—Yeah. If you could talk with Hendrickson that would be great.

—OK.

—Bye.

The minister was starting the sermon. I tried to tune in. His text was from Romans. *For all have sinned and fall short of the glory of God.* A good one for each of us. The phone rang again. Mr. Developer took the call. Tattoo boy sent a text to porn girl sitting next to him. Porn girl interrupted her conversation with momma to tell tattoo boy that she got his text. I got up and left.

I put the truck in gear and rolled slowly up the street to the top of the neighborhood. I passed through the open gate to the city water tank. I drove the gravel road to the top of the hill. I parked in the shade of a pinyon. I sat on the tailgate for a while. I swung my feet. I listened to the call of a wren. I heard the wind rattle some dry cottonwood leaves. I smelled the wind. I got back in the truck and went home.

I like to think of myself as a professional. But I'm not. I'm an amateur. I really am. Now. Detroit. Professionals. Writ large.

Motown. Two million people living there after the war. World War II. By the time the Great Recession was over almost three quarters of them were gone: A city declining towards half a million. Bankrupt. Empty. Derelict. A hundred square miles of abandoned buildings. Fifty thousand homes. A hundred thousand homes. Dumped. Abandoned. A ghost town. Life: Cheap: Murders. Car-jackings. Thefts. Burglary.

Somebody had to do something. So the mayor launched the Blight Removal Task Force. It is a mouthful I admit. But the sons-a-bitches were house breakers. Twenty thousand per year was the target. I'm not kidding. If you were on that task force you were a house breaker. Bonafide. They had 80,000 abandoned houses on their list the day they started. Deconstruction and demolition. That is what they called it. And it ain't bad as far as job descriptions go. I should know.

Unfortunately for Detroit they only had the recycling capacity for 1200 or 1400 buildings per year. They had to scale back. The whole thing was going to take 50 years. But. On the good side. It created jobs. It was a new industry. The deconstruction industry. A career. You could be a skilled deconstructionist. It wasn't just for Nietzsche anymore. Or Derrida. Or whomever.

Another name for it. A third thing to call it. In Detroit they said that they were removing blight. Out here in Box Elder County they've been creating it. Creating blight. And at about the same rate too. Seems like an opportunity for arbitrage. How about a blight moving business? Buy low; sell high. I'm a goddamn blight hauler. Load it in Detroit; offload it in the New American West.

But. Seriously. I should go there. Right? I mean. Detroit. That is the place for me. Heaven for house breakers. There is probably a college for house breakers. A grocery store. Broken Foods. Har. Girls. Probably female house breakers. Easy for a house breaker to get a date. A whole house breaking community. House breaker cocktail parties.

—Wadjew dew today?

—Oh man. Finally got the last of the sheathing into the dumpster.

—Yer kicking my ass man. I'm still working on the damn siding.

—What kind?

—Asbestos.

—Oh hell. Bad luck dude.

I even heard that the mayor was considering proposals for what to do with the land. I mean. They are going to have ten thousand acres of vacant land. Or more. Twenty. Thirty thousand. The mayor is taking proposals.

Forests says one group. Plant trees. Forests like LaSalle saw. Marquette. Radisson. I don't know about Detroit. But usually. In Michigan. If you do nothing the forest comes on its own. Jack pine. Aspen. Balsam fir. Red maple. Ironwood. Red pine. Hemlock maybe. Basswood.

Gardens says another group. Local food for local consumers. Locavors. Foodies. We'll make this a haven for the fresh food crowd. Hipsters. Hippies. Beards. Grow local; eat local.

Actually. None of these ideas are new. I thought of them first. I'm already implementing them. Break the house; plant a garden. Detroit is simply copying me.

But this isn't Detroit. This is the West. This is the New West. The New American West. The west of freeways. Of house flippers and back yard chickens. Of flip flops and tattoos. Of seeker-sensitive churches and tax breaks for developers. Of cell towers and satellite TV. Fucking TV. The west of convenience stores and dollar stores. Of ATVs and UTVs. Escalades and Audi Quattros.

This is not the old west. The west of Jed Smith. The west of John C. Fremont or Kit Carson. Not the west of Brigham Young or Willa Cather. Not the west of Herbert Bolton or Ann Hafen. This is not the west of Ivan Doig. This is not even the west that I remember: The west of scruffy rural towns. Dumpy diners and dirty bars. Full of farmers and tractor mechanics. The kind who could either fix you up and get you on the road or give you a place to sleep in the barn.

One time I bought a 1966 Ford for a friend in Cottonwood. I mean. I bought the truck in Cottonwood; the friend was elsewhere. I was headed for Boise with it and I made it past Riggins—I think—before it quit. I got it going again and limped it into some little town—New Meadows, Council, Cascade, Cambridge?—before it quit again. This time for good. It was after business hours but I was able to find a mechanic to help me. He came in—drunk—to his shop. Night was fast approaching. He figured out that I was sucking rust from the bottom of the old gas tank and that the rust was fouling the engine. Working together we pulled the gas gauge out of the tank and went in through the gauge hole to rig a filter and tube system that by-passed the plugged fuel lines.

When we were done he wouldn't take any money. Instead. He went to a 1950s era refrigerator and retrieved two bottles of beer. One for me; one for him. We drank them in a couple of pulls. We shook hands. Then I spent the night behind a Grange Hall. On the front seat of the truck. My face stuck to the vinyl. The persistent smell of gasoline in my nostrils.

I woke in the cold dawn—stiff and swollen eyed. I got the truck going and found a greasy spoon. Open at 5:30. The waitress grabbed the Folgers off the Bunn warmer without looking at me. She poured into the cracked white china cup without a word—the thin brown liquid arcing 18 inches from the carafe to the mug. I had eggs and toast for $2.50. I sat there and tried to collect my wits. I could hear a couple of old boys in the booth behind me.

—You might could get Pete to steer the truck while you and the boys tossed the bales.

—Yeah. Might.

The waitress kept my coffee full. A few truckers came in. I sat vacant eyed. The warm café. The quiet hum of voices. A waitress. After a while I started to feel better. I decided to go out. To see if the truck would start again.

It's not like that anymore. Not in the New American West. If you break down in the new west you better make sure you're clear of the lane. The speed limit says eighty but we're crowding ninety and god help you if you get in our way.

Even in the back-country. Fast. Drive fast. Modern sport utes can handle it. They really can. Amazing. Excellent engineering. Especially the Subarus. Toyotas. Hammer 'em. Rough rocky terrain. Here they come. Up behind you. Cool as shit. Got it made. Growing hair under the lip. Fancy gear piled on the roof. Thirty miles per hour. Forty.

You're out in the woods. Getting wood. For the stove. Old truck. Loaded half way up the racks. Windows open. Sweat drying. Making your way. Here they come. Sportmobiles. Mountain bikes. Kayaks. Rafts. Snowboards. Ain't nobody got to work in the New American West. It's just a playground now. Get the hell out of our way.

4

Glory brought out some lemonade for us and sat down with us, and we talked a little bit about television. Your mother has been looking at it, too. I don't enjoy it myself. It's not the last impression I want to have of this world.

Marilynne Robinson

On Monday I called the gas company and asked for service to be disconnected. It seemed like a simple request. It must happen sometimes. Right? Evidently this gas company representative hadn't heard of it. Or was unable to deviate from the script.

—Sir. While I have you on the phone we are offering paperless billing.

—That's OK. I called to have my service disconnected. I won't be needing anymore billing.

—I understand. Can I interest you in an energy audit? This service is completely free and will provide information about how to make your home more efficient.

—I'm planning to tear it down. I'm not worried about efficiency. Can you disconnect the service?

—Sir?

—I'm calling to have my gas service disconnected. You can do that?

—I'm sorry. I'll have to ask my manager.

He was gone for a few minutes. I listened to a tune that used to be Hotel California. This was a much more soothing version than the original. Much.

—Sir?

—I'm still here.

—To reconnect your gas service will require you to pay a service fee.

—I'm not calling to reconnect. I am calling to disconnect.

—I understand. But before you disconnect your service I am required to inform you that there will be a charge for reconnecting it.

—Thank you for the information.

—Now. Can I have your billing address?

—For what?

—For the disconnection service fee.

I didn't call about the satellite TV. Fucking TV. I don't know how those things work. And I certainly wasn't going to try talking to those idiots. Besides. I'd already recycled the dish. The bill for disconnecting that service could go to the Ewells.

At least the dish was small enough for me to cut down and throw away. Remember the first TV satellite dishes? They were the size of a farm silo and required a concrete pad to install. I don't know. They probably cost somewhere in the low- to mid-four figures—maybe more. But everybody had them. And for what? Fifty-seven channels (and nothin's on). Sorry Bruce. They were an eyesore. And if you wanted to get rid of one you had to just about hire a highway construction company. With a crane.

The ones you get now can hang on your RV. That's the thing that kills me. You can be out of work. Broke. Evicted. Living in gramma's camper behind the garage. But you've got a dish. By god. TV. Yeah. Fucking TV. Can't pay my rent but I got satellite TV.

But I don't mean to pick on trailer trash. Everybody does it. Buy a second home. Out by the lake. Out in the woods. At the beach. Condo at Tahoe. Where ever. What is the first thing? Get a satellite dish.

—How was yer vacation?

—Great.

—Wadja do?

—Watched TV.

Fucking TV.

Build a cabin. Your own Innisfree—a bee-loud glade. Can't hear the bees. The TV is on. Speaking of Innisfree. What is it that the poet does there? He lives alone—in peace. Solitude. And peace. Two things not allowed by the TV.

The house breaker doesn't have a lot of friends. To be good at house breaking requires a bit of a contrarian outlook. You may be going against the grain sometimes. It can be hard for people to understand. Than again. Maybe it is just me. I am admittedly anti-social. It is possible that other house breakers are party animals. I just don't know any: Other house breakers. I've never been to Detroit.

Actually. There was one old place over by the elementary school. It was a mess. Probably a rental. Trash in the yard. Old vehicles. An old school bus. I would sort of drive by and look at it once in a while but I never did see anyone. The thing was it was an older style wooden frame house. It was one of those old semi-victorian little miner's shacks or something. Probably 60 or 80 years old. Or more. I thought it might have some potential. Not for breaking but for fixing. I mean it had wooden clapboards for god's sake. I know they're a pain in the ass. You've got to paint them and all. But this wasn't just a plastic box. Somebody had actually built it.

After a while though the renters must have moved out. Pretty soon the windows were broken. The door kicked in. I still thought it had potential. I could see some old pine floors in there and some unfinished woodwork. And a lot of beer cans.

Then there was a track-hoe in the yard. It had a thumb. With the thumb the track-hoe was picking up pieces of the house and putting them in a huge dumpster. Somebody was breaking a house. Not the way I'd do it. Not the right kind of house. But at least they weren't going to let it sit there and decay. Pretty soon it was all gone and the lot was clear.

Actually. Just after buying the Ewell house I made a friend. One friend. A person at work. Michelle.

There were fifteen or twenty people sitting in a staff meeting listing to our director. He liked to hear himself talk. He talked a lot. I tried not to pay attention. I had a notebook on my lap. I studied it and scratched some notes. It was a list of things that I needed to do on my house project. After a while I realized that the director was talking about the Ottoman Turks and the Armenians. Was it a manuscript he had picked up? Or was it simply outrage from something he'd heard on NPR? Stupid NPR—smug and self-righteous. I tried to tune him out again but was less successful. After pontificating about genocide for a few minutes the director concluded with some numbers. Over a million Armenians systematically exterminated—maybe a million five. The director stopped abruptly. There were a couple of beats of silence. I'm not sure anyone had been listening. I quietly said the first thing that came to my mind.

—So it goes.

There was more silence. Maybe it was embarrassed silence? Certainly no one laughed. Even though it was funny. I mean it wasn't ha-ha funny. But it was funny the way it was funny that allied bombers burned Dresden to the ground on the night of February 13, 1945 killing tens of thousands. Hundreds of thousands? It was also funny that no one seemed to get it. I mean the job is publishing. Are people who work in publishing illiterate? Probably. I kept my head down. I worked on my task list. I heard a little noise. It sounded like a giggle. I glanced down the table. A woman was looking straight at me. Michelle. Her eyes were bright.

When the meeting was over I stopped at the side table to top off my coffee. As I turned away someone gave me a light hip-check. It was Michelle.

—Billy.

She smiled at me again.

—Billy Pilgrim.

She walked away.

The next morning she stopped at my office on her way to the copier and asked how I was doing. We talked briefly. She called me Billy. It was slightly annoying. But I guess I'd asked for it.

Illium has several imprints. Some of them make good profits; others of them make good books. I am only half kidding. I work for Voyageur. We are probably modestly profitable. But our focus is on history and biography—mostly North American—so our authors are not commonly on the best seller lists. We publish serious but accessible works on a range of well-known—and some less well known—events and or people. We might—for example—accept a short biography of Maynard Dixon with a few color plates or a well-documented account of a modern historian following the Oregon Trail—a la Parkman.

I was—that autumn—working to put out a biography of Rauschenbusch—the late nineteenth and early twentieth century theologian. It was unlikely to be a big seller. But it was timely and well written. The bean counters thought it could at least break even.

From what I had heard Michelle had recently completed a Ph.D. in Art History. She had been hired several months ago by Voyageur to work on a number of artist biographies. From what I could tell she was a little younger than me. Plain but pretty. The title they gave her was "junior" editor. They gave her an office on the other side of the building from mine.

The bank hired a crew to clean up the Ewell house before listing it. They came over on a Saturday. I was at home. I could hear them over there. I walked over to watch. The foreman looked like John Candy. He shouted at a young Hispanic woman. He sent her into the house while he lazily wandered the property.

A young punk on a lawn tractor was mowing at top speed. There wasn't much grass. He was mowing the weeds and the trash. If there was something laying in the weeds he mowed over it. A board or a rock or a kid's toy. He didn't stop and get off. He didn't even slow down. There would be a loud crash. A few parts would fling out. He would keep going.

I saw a rock picked up by the mower blade and sent over the fence into the yard next door. Fortunately no one was there. It made a certain amount of sense. Mulching the trash made for less to be picked up. You certainly couldn't be expected to remove the small stuff. Make it all small stuff.

I watched Candy poke around at the chicken coop. He wasn't much of a help to his crew. He really wasn't. He stuck his hand in the coop to reach for something. Whatever he grabbed had a wasp's nest on the bottom. A wasp stung him. He dropped the object like a hot potato and started swinging his hand back and forth. At first I felt sorry for the guy. I mean nobody likes being stung. But the more I watched he and his crew the less I cared. A bunch of lazy thugs. They could all be stung for all I cared. In fact I hoped they would.

That's the thing about me. I don't go out of my way to injure people. But it doesn't bother me if pure laziness and stupidity lead to someone's misfortune. I sort of wish it on them too. I know it doesn't sound very good. But I've already admitted to being a jerk. Besides. I'm an equal opportunity jerk: My own misfortunes are usually the result of laziness or stupidity. Or both.

I skipped church for a couple of weeks. It's not really the fault of the church or anyone in it. I mean there are half-dressed slobs and loud talkers wherever you go. At the airport. In the grocery. The post office fer god's sake. Slouching along with guts hanging over the baggy shorts. On the phone. I don't know what it is. People don't really care to be quiet and self-contained. They feel comfortable hanging it all out there—feet and flesh and conversations featuring a one word vocabulary—fuck. Fuckin' fuckers. Honestly I don't want to know about your miserable business. But I can hardly help it.

I was at the public library last week. Guy there doing some lawyering for some poor old bastard—veteran. The guy was loud. The pseudo-attorney.

—I said to that lady at the VA. You better not hang up on me. Cause I'll tell you what. That'da been me. I'da killed that doctor. Strangled him right there. What'd ya mean it wasn't agent orange? I got a brain tumor.

The veteran murmured something agreeable. Poor bastard. He probably needed the guy's help. But he was embarrassed to be sitting there with him. The guy was a real know-it-all. A show off.

—Now. In your case. If you had a record of the first time you experienced the loss of vision we could get you 20 years of back-pay. Just think about it. Get me a date. I don't care if I have to go in front of that VA judge and grab him by the collar. There is no way we lose this case.

Like I say. The problem isn't the church. (Or the library.) The problem is me. I just don't like it. My ideal is silence. Maybe a place where you can think. But it is foolish to expect that. Church. Library. Post Office. They are just places where we all do what we all do. They are places for us to express ourselves. Like we do everywhere else.

But I'm an irritable guy. I can have a bit of a temper. And it makes me angry to listen to people talk on their phone in church. So sometimes I skip it. Church I mean. There is no sense going to church to get pissed off. I have plenty of opportunities for that during the week.

5

I have finally taught Dean that he can do anything he wants, become mayor of Denver, marry a millionaires, or become the greatest poet since Rimbaud. But he keeps rushing out to see the midget auto races.

Jack Kerouac

A house breaker doesn't break just any house. It has to be affordable for one thing. You can't really break a house you don't own. You have to buy the house first. Then you can break it. If you want.

It has to be ugly. You break houses that were thrown together in six weeks. Dull soulless boxes. Unsuitable for human habitation. All plastic and vinyl. Ugly. Built cheaply. Built carelessly. Built in a hurry. Built to fall apart.

Abandoned. The owners were lazy. They let the cheap plastic house fall apart—vinyl siding stained and chipping. They didn't pay the bills. The bank foreclosed. They moved out. Left all the trash. The yard full of thorns and weeds. The driveway cracked and covered with spilled oil.

Or maybe a low-rent rental. Loud cars coming and going all the time. The constant thump-thump of hip-hop through the walls. Noisy. Barking dogs. Pit bulls. A couple of dirty kids. Furniture on the yard. Smoking a cigarette in the doorway. Flip the butt. Flip a couple hundred butts. Thousands.

The house that I live in was flipped. It is a handsome one hundred year old sprawling hand built farmhouse. The old boy living here had diabetes. Couldn't quite handle it. Talk about run down. Big old high ceilings. Deep windows. Bright. Cold. He couldn't keep enough wood in the stove. He was buying from the sawed-off pick-ups in front of the Walmart. Flipper came to the door. Offered him cash. The old boy used the money to buy a little blue plastic box. He lives across town. I see him now and then. Struggling out of the car and shuffling up to the vinyl.

The flipper put some money into it. I mean it. Vomit brown carpeting over the pine floors. A furnace in a closet. With a thermostat. No need to put wood in the stove. Flop down in front of the TV. Fucking TV. The heat comes on. Another layer of ten-year shingles over the leaking roof. Don't fix the floor. Just roll some linoleum over it.

The flipper got some money out of it too. Subdivided. The old orchard was gone. Turned into a new lot. Big enough for somebody to build another piece of shit blue box. The horse corral was gone. A new lot. Big enough. He waited a year and sold 'em all. Got more than the lots were worth and sold the house to a young couple. The flipper used the money to buy a chateau. He lives out of town. I see him now and then. Shuffling from the Escalade to the mesquite wood door. I hate him. I hope he dies a slow painful death.

It has taken me almost ten years to put it all back together. I overpaid to get the orchard back—fortunately no one had built on it. Scraped vomit off the floors. Cut off the gas to the furnace. Replaced the roof. Bought the corral from the bankruptcy court. I guess I'm paying for that chateau. Live like a king on a pile of some else's debt. It's even got a tennis court. Who cares that a nice old homestead is gone to shit? Subdivided. Sold. Hell. Who am I to complain? To hate the flippers? It's a free country. Right? It is simply another way of doing business. I mean I guess I'd live in a chateau. A shateau.

This time Michelle sat directly across the conference table. I took my regular staff meeting pose—head down and notebook on my lap. It was pretty bad. I bet the director talked for ninety minutes straight. I worked very hard to keep from listening.

Finally the group got around to discussing the Christmas party. God. It was barely Halloween and we had to talk about Christmas. Christmas already? At the end of October? What ever happened to Thanksgiving? You know what happened to Thanksgiving: It never made anybody any money. Ever notice that? In a society built on consumption we have little tolerance for the holidays that can't be retailed. That is the problem with Thanksgiving. If you are thankful you can't hardly be expected to go buy anything. Oh sure. You gotta get the turkey and the stuffing and all that. But that ain't nothing compared to the Halloween costumes and Christmas orgy. So there is not a lot of mention of Thanksgiving anymore. Why talk about it? It is only important as the prelude to Black Friday. Yeah. Black

Friday. Now that counts as a national holiday. Black Plague is more like it.
And. Come to think of it a black plague would suit me just fine. A plague
on all y'all.

Anyway. A lot of people at Illium put a lot of effort into the Christmas
party so it takes several months of planning. I really hate it. Christmas is
fine but the office party is gruesome. Secret santas. White elephants.
Snowmen. Wisemen. Rudolf. It got me thinking about those horrible
nativity sets people are always putting in the yard. Vinyl camels and all that
crap. Inflatable even. Inflatable santas hovering over a vinyl Jesus.
Inflatable santas on inflatable Harleys delivering gifts for the wise men.
And some of them built to play Christmas carols. Over and over. Jingle
bells. Day and night. Nauseating.

Then I started thinking about something that happened in our town last
year: The vinyl baby Jesus went missing from the nativity set in front of the
library. The city council was not in the mood. They ordered the chief of
police to crack down. The top cop successfully tracked the thief to a local
home. He found Jesus in the back of some kid's little red wagon. I'm not
kidding. The kid had prayed for a wagon. He made a covenant with
God—a contract. Like the Israelites: The promised land for a promise of
faithfulness. You give me a wagon and I'll give Jesus the first ride. When
the kid got an early Christmas present he had a debt to pay. I bet Jesus
loved that. A break from manger duty for a ride around town in a red
wagon. Even if it did last for a couple of days. It would have been better
than sitting in that stupid nativity scene with santa filling the sky like a cloud
and the constant upbeat jingle of jingle bells. Anyway I don't think the city
prosecuted the wagoner but he did have to give up his passenger. Back to
the manger for Jesus.

In the middle of all the discussion around the conference table I
suddenly heard someone say:

—Look. I have to know. Are you or aren't you coming over to help
me trim the tree Christmas Eve?

My head snapped up. It was Michelle. She was looking at me—her lips
curled in a conspirator's smile. I looked down. It made me nervous. What
was she doing? I wanted to get out of there.

—I mean I have to know.

It seemed like the meeting was over. I slipped out of my chair and
headed for the door. I didn't know what was going on. I'm not very good
at understanding girls. Women. Was she sending me a message? Was she
half crazy? I mean she couldn't be sending me a message. What if she
intended for me to hear that? I mean she must have intended me to hear
that. Why? Did she want me to notice her or something? It made me sort
of nervous thinking about it.

It is not as though I've never had a girlfriend. I've had a few girlfriends. Not a lot. I guess I'm not real smooth with girls. But I like them. I like having girlfriends. Mostly they don't really like me though. I mean I'm not bad looking. I'm not. And I can pay my bills. I'm not a deadbeat. I went to college. Even grad school. I've got a job and can more or less function in the world. But I have kind of a short temper. I'm set in my ways. I can be pretty irritable. It's true. I can be kind of a jerk sometimes. I know who I am and what I like. I'm not going to change. It seems like a lot of girls want you to change.

Take Julia. I went around with her for six months or a year. I really liked her. I did. We had some great times together. She was fit and liked to be outdoors. We'd go on hikes or toss the Frisbee or go out to the lake. She was smart too. That girl really had some brains. It was fun. We talked a lot. Everything was fine. It really was. But I started noticing that she wanted me to maybe wear some nicer clothes and pay about $20 for a haircut. I jokingly paraphrased Jack Burden for her once: As the pressure to improve my grooming increases so my resistance increases. I'm not sure she thought it was very funny. And pretty soon we were having a lot of serious talks about the future. She wanted to make sure we'd have a nice place to live and maybe go to some better restaurants. She wanted me to have a better job. Maybe go to law school. It wasn't that she was a gold-digger or anything. I mean she was smart and hard-working herself. She just wanted to be part of an ambitious dual-income couple.

I remember Julia and I finally had this knock-down-drag-out. At one point she was insisting that I give her a target income range for my future career—how much did I expect to earn in the next ten years or twenty. I honestly don't think she cared that much about being rich or anything. I think she just wanted a certain social status. And I didn't blame her. I really didn't. I could see how she thought it would be nice to be one of those couples with really respectable careers and a solid monthly income— going on nice vacations and driving up-to-date cars. Listening to NPR. Stupid NPR. I just didn't understand how she thought I was going to be part of that. This was before I took up house breaking. But even then I was pretty low-end. I was generally happy with an old truck and a cord of wood on the porch. And I'd never pretended otherwise. That was the thing that really bugged me. I was just that way when we met. And I was just that way when we'd been together for six months. Why did she think I was ever going to be anything other than that? How did Sal Paridise put it? *She wanted me to be her way.* It's not like I'm really a slob either. I get out of bed every day. Have a shower. Put on clean clothes.

Anyway we had this big talk and I started to get pretty irritated after a while. I wasn't exactly shouting. But I was being a bit of a jerk. Finally I told her that I thought we should take a break from each other. She didn't disagree. Not for a second. She grabbed her keys and went out the door. I never actually saw her again. Old Julia. After two or three months I tried to call her one time. But she didn't call me back. I dropped it.

At work the next day I was sitting at my desk. My office door was open. Michelle came and leaned against the jamb. She just looked at me.

—Sally.

She smiled.

—Sally Hayes.

She laughed.

—I knew you'd get it.

Then she walked away. I just sat there. I still had no idea what to think.

6

[B]efore a town can have buildings or prosperity or any of those
things, some realtor has got to sell 'em the land? All civilization starts
with him. Jever realize that?

Sinclair Lewis

After getting disconnected the first task was the dumpster. I meant to
salvage as much as I could from the house. I planned to continue recycling
the metals. I planned to save the lumber. I planned to have a yard sale or
two. I planned to keep some hardware. Keep doors. Sell windows. But.
No matter what. House breaking makes trash. Used sheetrock. Used
insulation. Used carpet. Used siding. I mean. There are some things you
can do. But you're going to throw a lot of it away. The best solution is a
roll-off dumpster. The waste management guys drop it in your yard. You
fill it. They dispose of the trash.

It's not cheap. Renting a dumpster I mean. The big companies can
charge three to five hundred bucks to rent a 30-yard dumpster for a week
or two. If you need it longer than that they might charge you an extra ten
dollars a day.

I was able to get more of a local deal. One of the excavating guys in
town has a couple of dumpsters. A little sideline. Bobby. I wanted to keep
one over the winter. Five or six months. So I called Bobby. Winter is a
slow time in the dumpster business. Bobby said I could have one for a few
months. A hundred a month.

He brought it over and dropped it near the house. At one end of the
house. Funny guy. Old Bobby. Looks like he's 85 years old. And
probably he is. But he goes around in a dump truck. An excavator. A

back hoe. He's hauling gravel. Hauling dirt. He's got his blasting license. Only guy in the county. An old style powder monkey. Busy. Always busy. You'd think he'd be a millionaire by now. And maybe he is. But he doesn't look like it. Doesn't act like it. Always giving a guy a deal. I had to have my entire sewer line replaced one time. Probably a $6000 job. He came. He worked like a mule. He did a great job. He went away. He came back with a bill. $2,100. Could hardly have covered his fuel. Maybe that's why he's not a millionaire. A lot of loyal customers though. Nobody in town will use anybody else.

—Thanks Bobby. That looks great.

—Looks like it needs a new roof.

—Yeah.

—Fixing this one up?

—Well.

—Gonna do to it like you done over there?

—Yeah.

—Interesting hobby if you can afford it.

He buzzed. It was a phone. An incoming call. It was for him. He pulled out a cell phone. A nice one. A smart phone. An iphone. Here was a guy who might have been born before they had land lines. Talking on a smart phone. Like he'd done it his whole life. Funny guy. Old Bobby. He looked at the screen. He looked at me.

—It's my daughter.

—Oh.

—Hello. Yeah. Yeah. OK.

He hung up. Looked at me again.

—Gotta go. Call me when you're done with the dumpster.

—Yeah. Great. Thanks Bobby.

There is really no way to keep up with them. The developers. The realtors. The flippers. At best I can break one house every two years. Two years? Heck. Even a small-time builder—on half an acre—will be ahead of me four to one. And most of them are no longer small-time. I don't know. Maybe they can build one per week. No matter how you figure it I'm fighting a losing battle. And it is hard to find help. Entering the business is expensive and the profits are strictly long term.

So why do it? Why break houses? Really. Who would?

About the only answer I can give is that it is a way to diffuse my anger. I'm not saying I'm right but trash makes me angry. I can sit in my fury or I can get up and clean the trash off the lot next door. I can't stop the flow of trash—the city council recently approved construction of a dollar store not three blocks from my house—but I might be able to remove it from my immediate view.

Breaking the Ewell house gives me a task. Channels my anger. Gets my mind off the noise. Plus. It gives me another hundred feet of elbow room.

I should probably move. Go somewhere. Somewhere empty and ugly. Somewhere unattractive to bourgeois bohemians. Unattractive to yuppies. Unattractive to developers. Is there such a place? Unattractive enough not to attract the men who can ruin anything. Developers can ruin anything. A dump. Developers could ruin a trash dump. But. Anyway. Go. There should be someplace unwanted enough to be quiet. Just the sound of the wind. Maybe a wren. Detroit. No one wants Detroit anymore. Right? Do they have wrens in Detroit?

The problem. And believe me I've thought about it. The problem is that I love the hard clean light of the southern Rockies; I love the sudden cold rush of dusk along the Seedskadee; I love the thought of Hite there in the mud where used to be a river. It would be difficult to leave. To go away from the light and the sky. Like A.B. Guthrie, Jr. had it: *Give him a far reach of eye, the grasses rippling, the small streams talking, buttes swimming clear a hundred miles away.*

After Julie there was Sherri. Sherri was not ambitious; she didn't have to be. She was wealthy and popular from the start. Her parents owned a ski shop and high-end restaurant at a ski resort. I ended up there for a season after graduate school. I bumped chairs for a ski pass and paid enough rent at a buddy's dump to take possession of what was essentially a closet. I had a mattress on the floor and one meal a day. Those were my ski bum days I guess.

Sherri drove a Range Rover and lived in her own log home. She was beautiful—well put-together and dressed to prove it. She'd grown up skiing. She was fit. Outgoing. Rich. Posh. I don't know. Not like anything I'd ever seen.

I knew who she was. Everybody did. I bumped her chair at the lift.

One day I was skiing by myself. I dropped off a steep hill into some brush made two turns and stopped. I looked for a line through the oak. There was someone standing there. I recognized Sherri. I said hi. She said hi. I pushed off and worked my way to the bottom. I stopped there and looked back. Sherri skied my line. Skied it beautifully. She stopped near me.

—Great day, huh?

—Yeah.

She skied away. But after that she acted like she knew me. She'd ski the lift where I was working and make small talk at each chair. One night I saw her at the bar. There was a live band. People were dancing. She came up and took my hand. We danced together. She was wearing a tight low-cut top. She had beautiful breasts. After a while she lead me out to her Range

Rover and took me to her house.

In the morning she bought me breakfast at a busy café and began a serious talk.

—I'm falling in love. I can't stop thinking about you.

—Uh-huh.

—I feel like we've had this connection from the first time we saw each other.

—Yeah.

—Love at first sight I guess.

She laughed. I laughed too. It was ridiculous. It really was. We had nothing in common. We'd barely met. But I didn't bother to argue. I was—after all—a dirt-bag liftie in a high-end ski town. I couldn't even pay for my own bagel. And here she was—rich and gorgeous—sitting there telling me that we were soul mates. Who was I to quibble?

Sherri was a woman who was in love with being in love; a woman who needed novelty romance excitement. She liked new things; she liked secret things; new secret things. For a while I was the new thing. I was exciting and different. We had secrets. Secret ways of looking at each other and secret ways of being together. She was thrilled. And thrilling.

I remember one time we went away together for a weekend. A three-day weekend. On the road. To Albuquerque. Or somewhere. El Paso. We signed ourselves in as Mr. and Mrs. Smith. We ate at good restaurants. We skinny dipped in the pool. And everything was more exciting than it had ever been—we were the last couple in the universe. Like. I don't know. Like Gatsby and Daisy. Or something. Someone.

But. Of course. But. It was never going to last. Did it for Gatsby? I don't know that I was bored. But I was certainly dissatisfied with being a bum. We went around together for six months. In that whole time I never paid for so much as a piece of bubble gum. Sherri let me drive the Range Rover but she paid for all the gas. I don't know. Maybe some guys would like it that way but I needed something of my own. I needed an occupation. An identity. Something that I did for me. I wasn't going to be Sherri's toy forever. Besides. She wasn't going to tolerate me forever. Pretty soon I was going to lose my novelty. I was going to be just another deadbeat ex-boyfriend. We were on a dead end street.

I started applying for jobs. I took the first offer that came my way and moved on. The night before I left was a final opportunity for excitement. Sherri gazed into my eyes and recounted the many high points of our love. She then removed her clothing and created a new one.

Old Sherri. Gorgeous woman. Popular. Rich. Beautiful. But not really interested in me. Interested in the excitement of a new romance. Which she—of course—had no trouble locating: Two weeks after I moved out of her house one of my ski bum buddies told me that she was engaged to someone else. Engaged! It hurt a little I suppose. But I wasn't really surprised.

I saw her one time after that. Sherri. I was at a summer arts and music festival in her home town—the ski town. I was hanging around with some of the old ski bum guys. We ran into Sherri on the street. She was with a couple of female friends but came directly to me and gave me a long hug. We became momentarily separated from the rest of the gang. She kept her hand on my arm and gazed into my eyes. We had a secret time together there on the edge of the crowd. A sixty second love affair:

—It is so good to see you.

—Uh-huh.

—You look great—handsome and strong.

—Oh. Thanks.

—I'm married now.

—I heard.

—But I'll always feel connected to you. I could feel it as soon as I looked at you today.

—You could?

—We'll always love each other.

We will?

When I tried to buy the Roundy house three or four years ago I had to do it through a local realtor. A bank owned it. A bank from Houston. Or Atlanta. They hired a local realtor to sell it. The guy who had the listing was a real prince. He really was. I mean aren't they all? Smart. It takes a lot of brain power to be a realtor. You really have to do your homework. It's not just about selling used cars. You've got to know something about property law. And you've got to know some loan officers. Yeah.

This stud put up the sign. He took some pictures. He wrote up a listing. Good work. Except that the listing was wrong. It had the place on a .7 acre lot. There are some big lots in that neighborhood. But not that big. The house was actually sitting on a .35 acre lot with an empty lot beside it. Earl and Marlene had owned the vacant lot. So it looked like it was all together. But it wasn't. The bank only owned half of it. The half with the house.

The listing price was a joke. I decided to offer half. I went to the state's website and downloaded the "official" real estate contract. I wrote an offer. Cash. Signed it. Emailed it to the realtor. Then I called him. Nate. His name was Nate. Kid. Nate. You're a real prince. I mean it.

—Hello.

—Hi. My name is John. I'm trying to reach Nate Dow.

—This is Nate

—Hey. I just emailed you an offer for that house you've got listed for

Southern Bank. I'm calling to follow up.

—What?

—I made an offer on that house you listed for Southern Bank.

—What did you say your name was?

—John. John Smith.

—Are you a realtor?

—No.

—So how did you make an offer?

—I wrote what I was willing to pay on the state approved real estate contract and emailed it to you.

—Oh. (Pause.) Well that isn't the right form.

—What do you mean? It won't be accepted by the county when signed by both parties? It won't be accepted by the courts as a legal contract?

—No. I don't mean that. But the bank has another form that they require from buyers.

—Well perhaps you can fill out the bank's form from the information that I included on the contract. And just so you know the lot isn't .7 acres. My offer is for the .35 acres that the bank actually owns.

—My contact at the bank told me that they own the whole thing.

—Who is your contact? Perhaps I should speak with them.

—Well. They change all the time. I'm not sure who it is now. I think there is someone new.

—Have you been to the county to look at the plat map?

—No. But I have the listing from when the house sold last time. It says .7 acres.

—That's because the owners from last time owned two lots of .35 acres each. One of the lots had the house and the other was vacant. When they sold the house the new buyer did not buy the vacant lot. The bank only owns the lot with the house on it. The lot is .35 acres.

—I'll have to talk with my legal department.

—Who is your attorney? Perhaps I should speak with them.

—I don't know. They aren't in my actual office. I'll have to ask my boss.

—Who is your boss? Perhaps I should speak with him. Or her.

—Oh. No. Look. I'm taking my kid to karate practice. Can I call you tomorrow?

—Sure. Thanks Nate.

Nate. What a great guy. I mean it. He didn't call me the next day. Or the day after that. Hey. I'm patient. I mean we've all got things going on. Right? Like karate practice. If I tell you I'll call you tomorrow that means I've got a week. Right? Or a month? Or forever? Fuckin' Nate. May he be stung by one thousand wasps.

When I skip church I usually go out to the high desert country around town. Sometimes you can find a place where the wind blows and the lark calls and the red-tails hunt. If you're lucky it will be quiet. The motors will be silenced and the cell phones will be elsewhere. There aren't many places like that anymore.

Don't get me wrong. I'm no pagan. I'm not looking for God in a piece of sagebrush. Or in the track of a coyote. I'm not there to worship the golden calf. I'm just there to hear something. The same thing Elijah heard.

7

I got the city to disconnect the water and sewer. But I left the electricity on. I planned to use it to power my tools. And to light the house when I worked at night.

Of course. Everything was night now. It was early November and the days were short. By the time I left work each day the dusk was gathering and by the time I got to the Ewell house I needed lights.

On the way home on the first Tuesday of the month I stopped—in the dying light—at the elementary school. I went in through the door to the old gym—stage at one end—and showed my voter registration to the old lady at the desk. She found my name on the list and asked me to sign next to it. I signed. I went over and picked up a ballot. Paper. Still using paper ballots in this place. Which is fine with me. The real problem with paper is faced by the guy who wants to be a "write-in" candidate. Let me tell you something about being a write-in candidate: If your name ain't "Jones" you can forget about it. I mean. There was a guy that wanted me to write him in for mayor. I'd seen his flyer wrapped in the local paper. His name was Swindlehurst. I am not kidding. Nor am I politically astute. But I do know this: If your name is Swindlehurst you are not going to win a write-in campaign for political office anywhere in the country. I don't care if you are running for the office of dog catcher. And I've got nothing against Swindlehurst but I have no idea how to spell it.

Anyway. There on the ballot was the medical center expansion. A referendum. Described—naturally—by its boosters. Hard to vote against it. Hard to vote against a hospital. Jack up a few injuns living in hogans or whatever. Give 'em the two bits their shacks are worth and send 'em down the road. I mean. A couple of shacks as against a hospital? It wouldn't have stopped Willy Stark; and it wasn't going to stop Box Elder County either. The medical center expansion was going to pass in a landslide. I voted against it and moved on down to the city council members. I didn't know most of them and didn't want to. But I'd seen how one of the guys mentioned doing great things within the scope of the budget. All the rest of them skipped the part about the budget and talked only about doing great things. Not that it was going to matter in an up and coming place like Box Elder County but I voted for the guy who at least knew there was such a thing as a budget.

When I was done I started home. Started for the Ewell house. I planned to work for an hour. Get something done before building the fire in my house and making a sandwich. But I didn't go straight home. I needed some alcohol. Working at night requires alcohol. A bottle of wine. I needed a bottle of wine to keep me company. Sip a little wine. Drag a few broken doors and pieces of plumbing to the dumpster.

On that plan I stopped at the liquor store on the way home. I wanted a decent bottle of red. The shop was empty but for a scruffy looking older guy with a dense gray beard and dirty jeans. He was standing at the counter trying to get the attention of the tired looking lady behind the plywood. Barb. As I went down the aisle I heard him asking when the next shipment of Boone's Farm would arrive. Boone's Farm. No joke.

—I like the red the best.

—It has the highest alcohol content.

—Oh. I thought I was drinking it for the taste.

—No. It has the highest alcohol content. It has more alcohol than beer.

He thought for a moment.

I walked up and put a bottle of Cabernet on the board.

—No wonder I like it.

Barb gave a little giggle. I tried to smile. It was probably more like a grimace.

Hoping to build on his success he tried again.

—No wonder I like it.

I swiped my card and took the bottle to my truck. I could hear him as I went out the door.

—Sure. No wonder I like it.

The next day it was my turn to get lucky. I'd decided to ask Michelle out. I mean I had decided to see if she wanted to go for a hike or something. I figured that she'd decline. But I didn't know what else to do. She'd wanted to play that game with Billy Pilgrim and Sally Hayes. What was that about? I thought that the best way out of it was to pretend to move forward. If she'd been flirting I'd call her bluff. If not I wouldn't have to worry about it anymore.

—Have you been up Three Creeks?

—I don't know. Doesn't sound familiar.

—I'm going on Thursday. Wanna join me?

—Thursday is Thanksgiving.

—I've heard of it.

—You don't have plans?

—I'm planning to go to Three Creeks.

—I mean you don't have dinner plans?

—I like dinner. I plan to eat it on Thursday.

We were at work. We were in the lane between cubicles. It was awkward. It really was. I was sort of asking her out. We were standing where everybody could hear us. And I was being a little obtuse. She paused. She was starting to turn away. She looked doubtful. I was probably going to go to Three Creeks alone. Which was just as well.

—I probably can't do it Thursday. I'm busy.

I guess that was going to be it. She was turning. It was fine. It really was. I made light of it. I smiled. I said the first thing that came to mind. Maybe it was a mistake. Maybe not. Depends on how you look at it.

—Well. You can go on back to hell where you came from. You old wart hog.

Michelle froze. She really did. She just stood there looking the other way. Then she turned back to me. She took a step forward. She reached out and put her hand on my shirt. Her eyes were bright.

—What time were you thinking of going?

For a while there was a guy using the local airport to teach flight lessons. Helicopters. Helicopter flight training. Out of the blue. Literally. One day there was a helicopter hovering over my house. Helicopters are really loud.

I saw something about it in the paper. Local politicians. The mayor. Falling all over themselves to welcome the helicopter school. Industry. You know. Jobs. Taxes. Jet fuel sales. Good for the community and all that.

I agree. Jobs. Taxes. Get somebody to pay for all those nice cop cars. But I hate helicopters. Did anybody even think about it? The mayor? Helicopters are loud. Maybe nobody notices. Whup-whup-whup. Night and day. I guess the mayor can't hear it. He is probably watching TV. Fucking TV.

There is the highway of course. That is loud too. Sometimes it bothers me. And there is the joyriding on the street outside my house. Up and down and up and down. Fat punks revving the motor. Because they can. All it takes is your foot on the pedal. As G.K. Chesterton once said: *The streets are noisy with taxicabs and motorcars; this is not due to human activity but human repose.*

But helicopters? We're the helicopter training center of the world evidently. Or we were. I think the school is gone now. Jet fuel is expensive.

We'd agreed that I would meet Michelle at the office. That I'd pick her up in the parking lot. I didn't want to scare her by telling her I'd meet her at her house. I didn't care to know where she lived.

She had dinner plans with friends in the afternoon. Thanksgiving dinner. So we agreed to meet early for a morning trip to the mountain. I got to the office parking lot at seven o'clock. She wasn't there. I shut off the truck and did a circuit to check the tie downs on my canoe. Maybe she wouldn't come. It was still dark. It was chilly. Who would come out on a cold dark Thanksgiving morning to go for a float on a reservoir in the mountains with someone they didn't know? With Billy Pilgrim?

—Hey Claude.

She'd parked her little Toyota hatchback two spots down from me.

—I thought I was Mary Grace?

—I don't see anything that looks like a Mary or a Grace.

—I guess not. Well. If I'm Claude I guess you're Mrs. Turpin.

—The warthog from hell.

—Yeah.

Hell. Yeah. She looked like something. But it wasn't a warthog. She was tall and slender with curves in the right places. She was fresh-eyed from sleep and smiling at me. I looked away. I tried to put the thought of her out of my mind. At least that thought.

I'd left the passenger door open. She went around and threw her backpack on the seat. We both got in and I started the truck. We idled out of the parking lot in the dusky early morning. Neither of us said anything for a while. It was a good silence. But I was wondering about her.

—You have a Ph.D.?

—Yeah.

—In what?

—Art History.

—Oh. What period? What genre?

—Nineteenth century American. Realism. Impressionism. Landscapes. Portraits. Still lives. You know.

—Oh. You have a favorite painter?

—Well. I don't know. You know. I really like Granville Redmond. But I mean. People don't really.

—Yeah.

—You know what I mean?

—Yeah. He's pretty good.

—You mean you know who Granville Redmond is?

—Well. I guess so.

There was decent light when we got to the lake. I unstrapped the canoe and pulled it off the truck. We threw the paddles and lifejackets in the bottom. I dragged the canoe to the water. Michelle knew little about paddling it. But after few pointers she did alright. The lake was still. There was nobody around. We paddled in silence. Drip drip drip. Gurgle. Drip drip drip. Gurgle. It wasn't bad.

When we got to the little island I aimed at a spit of gravel off the point and beached the canoe. Michelle climbed out and pulled me up. We walked to the top of the island and sat in the clearing. The sun was warm. It was late November. But it was one of those years. A long warm autumn. The lake could be frozen. There could be a foot of snow. But. Not this year. Indian summer.

—If you're the art lady how do you know Flannery O'Connor?
—I don't know. The way I grew up I guess. I read all the time. A real book worm.
I laughed.
—Maybe you're Mary Grace?
—Maybe.
—Wellesley?
—Hah. No. Why do you?
—What?
—Know O'Connor?
—It's my job I guess.
—Right.
—I'm a real book worm.
She looked at me.
—I'll bet.
—It's what you do when you ain't got no friends.
—I'll be your friend.
—Uh-huh.
—Why don't you come with me to dinner?
—When?
—Tonight.
—Thanksgiving?
—You've heard of it?
—Where are you going?
—My roommate's parent's house.
—Who's your roommate?
—Sandy. She works in admin.
—At Illium?

—Yeah.

—OK. I know her. I didn't know you were roommates.

—Well. Housemates. She had a place. I needed something when I got to town.

—When?

—I moved here last summer.

—How's it working out?

—Good. Fine. I like it. Sandy is alright. We're different but we've become pretty good friends. She looks out for me.

—Invites you to Thanksgiving dinner?

—Yeah. Why don't you come? It would be fine. I'll just give her a call.

—Oh. No. Thanks. Really. Probably not for me. I've got some other stuff to do.

—Like what?

—Like pulling some molding off a few doors.

—What?

—Oh you know. Just a project I've got going.

On the way back I asked her where she was from. About her parents.

—Minnesota. My Dad is retired from the defense industry.

—What did he do?

—Buyer. He was a buyer. Procurement. You know parts and stuff.

—Mom?

—She didn't work when we were younger. Went back when we were all in high school.

—Defense too?

—No. At the church.

—She worked at the church?

—Still does. She's not retired. Just Dad.

—What church?

—It's Minnesota.

—Lutheran?

She laughed.

—Yeah.

—What does she do? What is her job?

—Business manager. You know. She kind of runs the office. Keeps the books. Pays the bills.

—Did you attend?

—What?

—The church. I mean is your family Lutheran?

—Yeah.

—You?

—I guess.

—What is there to guess about?

—Well. Nothing. I just. You know. It can be hard to tell people about your religion.

—Yeah.

—I mean. Maybe people think you're going to be judgmental or something.

—Yeah.

—It is an easy way to offend people.

—Yeah. But not me.

—You mean?

—I mean I don't care. I'm not going to be offended about that.

The thing about house breaking is that there is always something to do even when you don't feel like it. Once you get going the work sort of distracts you. You work through one room and on to the next. The pile of trim and door parts starts to collect in the garage. Pretty soon the evening is gone. Which is good. Especially when you kind of like a girl and are wondering if you should have gone to dinner at the roommate's parent's place.

8

I spent most of the weekend over there and got into the carpet. You know the carpet. It's in every cheap plastic house. Puke brown. Can't see the dirt. Don't have to clean up. Spill your dinner on it? Just leave it. There must have been a sale on brown carpet at the carpet mine.

Anyway. I don't necessarily mind carpet. Removing it that is. Get the corner started and give it a vigorous tear. Once you've got a whole side pulled free it pretty much gives up.

I started in one of the bedrooms. I used a razor blade knife to cut one of the corners. I got my fingers under it. I pried it up. It didn't want to come. I wiggled another finger in. I gave it a jerk. It tore loose from the tack strip. I grabbed the loose piece in both hands and wrenched it. It unzipped down the wall. When the whole piece was free I rolled it up and carried it out to the dumpster. Cheap used carpet is not for yard sales. It goes in the trash.

I went back and pulled up the underlayment. If the installer is glue happy it can be a pain in the ass. But this one was mostly loose. I cut it up. I pulled it out. It went into the dumpster.

I went back for the tack strip. That took a while. A bucket a hammer a small crowbar. Pound pry break. Throw the section in the bucket. Pound pry break. On my knees. All the way around the room.

When I was done I went back with a broom. I know it is stupid but I like to clean up after myself. I'm breaking this house. I'm tearing it down. I'm dumping it. But I don't like it to be dirty. I know. It's not normal. But like I say. House breakers are solitary people. For good reason.

And ragpickers. I guess we don't have them here. No need. Why would anybody pick trash for a living? It's dirty. It's difficult. We don't believe in work like that.

44

It's tough. I don't doubt it. Not something I'd want to do. But I admire them. Steaming piles of refuse. Recycled. By hand. It's a living. You feed your family.

Think what it would feel like to a ragpicker to come to the western United States? To Box Elder County? A used aluminum can is worth a penny. Good money. Pick all day. Make four or five bucks. It's a gold mine. An aluminum mine.

Everybody else can go to the convenience store. Get a suitcase of beer. In cans. Twelve cans. Eighteen cans. Thirty cans. Your choice. Drink it all. Dump the cans on the road. Sleep it off. Get up. Get an energy drink. Drink it on the way to work. Throw it out the window. Pop? Drink it. Throw the can on the ground.

Ragpickers will get it. Four dollars a day. A living. You feed your family.

Actually. I'm willing to do it too. It is stupid. Probably costs more than it is worth. But I enjoy it sometimes. I don't know. Perversity. I am perverse.

Out in the canyon. Walking down the road. Hiking. Looking at something. Pretty soon I bend over and pick one up. Stand it. Crush it. Put it in my pocket. Milwaukee's Best. The Beast. Two or three on the next curve. Bud Light. Pepsi. Arizona Iced Tea. Coors. The Silver Bullet. In the pocket. In a few minutes my pockets are full. Then my hands. Cache them. Keep going. Natural Light. Mountain Dew. Keystone. PBR. Icehouse. Thirty. Thirty five. Reach the truck. Empty my pockets. The cans go in a bucket in the back. I stop at the cache. The bucket is full. At home I put them in a bag. At the end of the month I've got 150. Maybe 300. The next time I see Roger he gives me three dollars on top of the five I earned from dirty iron. Eight. Eight bucks. Heck. It's enough to pay for something. What? My monthly trash pick-up fee. There. I pick enough trash each month to pay for my trash to be picked up.

There was a staff meeting on Monday. I sat where I always sit. I put my head down. I had brought a manuscript to read. At the last minute someone sat next to me. I didn't look up.

The director wanted to get some things straight. There was too much small talk around the office. Not enough production. The directors had been looking at all of Illium's imprints. We were under performing. Maybe too many people flirting in the halls. Making smart ass comments at the staff meeting. I don't know. I concentrated on not concentrating. It's tough. He said. You are all professionals. It is not like we can send you home with a bad report card or something. He gave a lame laugh. But. He continued. There needs to be some accountability. I mean. All the department heads agree. I've tried more of a hands off approach with this group. Thinking that you all would see that we've not been meeting our targets. But. I'm afraid that I'm—we're—not going to have that kind of freedom anymore. We. He said again. We're all in this together. We're a team. For starters. He said. Very sympathetic now. We're not discussing measures that will impact anyone's pay or leave. He laughed again. This is not that kind of emergency. But I'm going to suggest a few items that will serve to concentrate the minds. You know. Bring back an atmosphere of professionalism.

Concentrate the minds? Did he just say concentrate the minds? Wait. I thought. I'm not listening to this. I am reading a manuscript.

The lunch room has certainly become a place to congregate. Perhaps— at times—a detriment to the business of the office. We could have it closed during the day? You know. Just a reminder that we need to get back to our desks. Open it between 11 and two let's say? He paused. There was silence. Or. He went on. We could cancel the gym membership program? It may have been abused a time or two. I mean. He paused. There were a few groans at this. People. He started again. Work with me here. Like I said. We're all in this together. What do you all think would work?

Down the table a lady started talking. Prim. Giving suggestions. Her voice was steady and sure. A real brown nose. I was relieved. It covered me. Gave me some space for a whisper. I could whisper what came to my mind.

—I'm sorry. Sir. *That window glass was so spick and span I completely forgot it was there.*

I looked back at my manuscript. A second later I felt an elbow in my ribs. A poke. I gave a brief sideways glance. It was Michelle. Next to me. A hand over her mouth and a light in her eyes. Oh. I thought. It's her. I put my head down again. Looking at my manuscript. But not thinking about it. Not thinking about the ongoing discussion either. The discussion about which privilege we would forego. Instead my mind was on her. On the way that she looked in my canoe that day. Slender. Quick. Alert. Cheerful.

When the meeting ended. I went for the door. As fast as I could go. I heard her growl.

—McMurphy.

I went back to my office spun the chair and slapped the mouse to make the laptop come up. Michelle came in as I sat down. She sat too. In a spare chair along the wall.

—You know what makes that story so great?

—What story?

—Hey. You started it. Cuckoo.

—What makes it so great?

—McMurphy is Jesus Christ.

—Jesus Christ?

—Yeah. The savior of the poor and the blind. The guy who comes from another world to heal the broken in this one. And when the system rises to crush him he sacrifices himself for his followers.

—Interesting. I like it. Except for one thing.

—What?

—The story of Jesus Christ—at least for Christians—is the story of a resurrection. There is no resurrection in Cuckoo.

She was quiet for a moment. Looking directly at me. Her eyes alert. Thinking.

—It's true. Not exactly the same. But what about Chief? *I been away a long time.*

—Yeah. OK. Maybe there is a resurrection.

I liked it. I really did. It was an intriguing take on a masterpiece of American fiction. But mostly I liked her. I liked her literacy. I liked the way she sat there looking at me.

Oh. And did I mention the dog? The Ewells had a dog. A little yappy thing. They thought it was cute. Cute. Yeah. Lap dog. The kind that wears a sweater. Oh. I forgot. Part of the American uniform: Cut-off shirt. Shorts. Flip-flops. Yappy dog. Goes on the airplane with you in a suitcase. Rides on your lap in the car. On the dashboard. Can't see out. But I've got my goddamned dog.

(I remember being in the back country once. In the winter. Cold. Icy. Wind. Single digit wind chill. After climbing in a no name canyon I went back to my truck. It was parked by the pavement. Next to it was a jeep. Hipster. LA. Guy from LA. He told me himself. I didn't even need to ask. Girlfriend in yoga pants. On vacation. Going camping. This was a bitchin place. Yeah. Bitchin. They were going to camp. With their dog. A Chihuahua. Wrapped in a little blanket. They were insane. I left as soon as I could get away from them.)

For all that the Ewell's loved the dog it couldn't go to work with them. They'd put it in the yard during the day. It would bark. Yap. Bark. Whine. Bark. Yap. Bark and bark and bark and bark and bark. I was at work most days myself. But every once in a while I'd be home. Day off. Sick day. Something. I'd be home. The thing would bark its damn head off. Bark and bark and bark and bark.

They didn't care. I talked to them about it. They couldn't believe it. Not little Ava. The dog was named Ava. Goddamned dog. A couple of times I considered killing it. I could have gone over there during the day and kicked it to death. When I started thinking that way I got in the truck and went up the canyon for a couple of hours. The only good thing was that the Ewells took Ava in during the night. I didn't have to hear from her after dark.

Dog people are delusional. They think that their dogs are part of the family. Are more or less human. They think that everybody must love the dog. Or at least respect it. Treat it with the respect due a human being. I don't know what they do. Maybe they have the dog sit at the dinner table with them. And use the potty. Put the seat down when you're done Fido.

Or. Who was it? Suttree? After Wanda dies he wanders the city for a week. Finds the old guy on the crumbling porch with a fat shit-colored dog in his lap. *When I die he's going to come to sleep with me. We're going to be buried together. It's done arranged. It is. I want him just like this. What if the dog dies first? What? I said what if the dog dies first? I mean if the dog dies first are they going to put you to sleep? Why hell no that's crazy. I guess maybe you could just have him frozen. Keep him till the time came. Of course I could.*

I once had a dog person tell me that his neighbor had lost a dog. The neighbor felt as though they'd lost a child. Um. I've never had a child so I wouldn't know. But I mentioned the story to a guy with two kids and two dogs.

—Are you shitting me? Dogs? That guy better not say that to anyone who has actually lost a child. They'll tear his jugular out with their bare hands.

At about that time I went to a conference. For work. The conference was held in a resort hotel. A lodge. I'm not talking about the crappy boxes built along the freeway with walls made of paper. This place had pretentions. Knotty pine woodwork and all. The conference ended on Thursday evening; I was planning to drive home on Friday morning. It was about a five hour drive. After the final presentation I went across the plaza to a little pizza place and bought a take-out pizza. I was planning to eat it in my room with a little wine and a good book. As I closed the door to my room I heard a loud yap. A bark. Somewhere nearby. Almost in the room. I froze. I stood there holding a pizza in a cardboard box. I was still for a couple of seconds. It was quiet. I took a step. Yap. Yap yap yap yap yap yap. The barking was coming from the room next door. It was one of those set-ups with a pair of doors between the rooms so you could rent them together and have the kids in one and mom and dad in the other. I walked to the interior door and listened to the snuffing and barking probably not three inches away. I also heard some muffled pleading. It was a woman's voice. Trying to quiet the dog. The dog—of course—ignored it. The dog was in charge. It usually is. I looked at my watch. It was about 6:30 pm. I turned around and walked to the other door—the door to the hallway. On the way I picked up my computer bag. My laptop. I went out and down the staircase to the outside. I walked to the parking lot and put the pizza and computer in my truck. I went back to the lodge and up the stairs. As I walked down the hall to my room a dog began to bark at me from under one of the doors on the other side of the hall. I opened the door to my room and stepped in. Immediately the yapping started up from behind the door to the adjoining room. There was no sound of human pleading anymore. Evidently the owner had given in to the inevitable. It took me a few minutes to throw some dirty underwear into my bag and pack up a couple of books. The dog yapped the whole time. Between yaps I could hear barking from across the hall. I scanned the room one last time and went out. I went back to the truck and put my bag and book box into the back seat. I walked around the corner of the building and through the front door. The lobby. I walked to the reception desk. There was no one waiting. There were two people behind the desk. Neither of them looked up. They were quite busy. Important job that. Checking people into the lodge. I went and stood in front of one of them. I dropped my key card on the counter. A heavy-set thirty-something lady in a lodge uniform.

—Can I help you sir?

—Do you have a pet policy?

—I'm sorry sir?

—Do you have a pet policy? Do you allow pets?

—Yes sir.

—Well. It is a bad policy.

—Is there a problem sir?

—There are two dogs on the second floor—rooms 244 and 247—that are currently barking their heads off.

—Oh. I'm sorry sir. I can have one of our people go up there and ask the owners to quiet the dogs.

—It won't do any good. The owners are unable to manage the dogs. The dogs do as they like. It is a bad policy. If you want to run a kennel that is fine. But this is a hotel. For people. People can't stay here if they have to have a dog barking in their face.

—I'm sorry sir. Is there anything else I can do for you?

I turned around and went out the front door. I went to my truck and drove out to the freeway. I got home at about 11:15 pm. I went back and forth to the truck twice for my gear. The yard was quiet. The Ewell's Ava was in the house. At 11:30 I sat down in my own kitchen and ate two or three pieces of pizza.

Like I said. Dog people are delusional. Believe it or not I don't want Fido's snout in my balls. I don't want dirty paw marks on my shirt. I don't want step in your fucking dog-person's shit. I don't want to listen to Fifi bark at me in my $300-a-night hotel room. Because no matter how much you think that animal is part of the family it still shits on the grass and pees on my tires. Get in touch with reality.

I don't really like to think of myself as a church shopper. But I guess that is what I am. I mean I believe in the Apostles Creed and all that. But it is hard to find a place to go. How does Percy's Tom More put it? *I believe in God and the whole business but I love women best, music and science next, whiskey next, God fourth, and my fellowman hardly at all.*

I tried again with the California come-as-you-are place. I'd only had one bad experience there. Of course it was my only experience there. But I thought I could try the other side of the building. I slid into a seat near the back. There was nobody else in the row. There was a group of people in the row in front of me. They were talking. But they quieted down OK when the service started.

Then the pastor got to what the bulletin called "passing the peace." In a traditional service you are supposed to say something about peace. May God's Peace Be With You. In a California come-as-you-are service it is another opportunity for talking. About yourself. I mean why else are we here. This is all about me. Right?

The burly guy in front of me turned around. Tattoos. Shorts. Oh. Surprise. The American uniform. Where is the dog? I recognized him. He was the greeter from the last time I'd attended the church. His name was Cory. He stuck out his hand. Big fake smile. I took it.

—Hey Cory.

Slight pause. A little less of a smile.

—Hey Buddy.

I could tell he had no idea where he'd seen me. I love how these douche bags call everybody buddy. It is easier than remembering someone's name. Remembering someone's name means less room in the brain for thinking about oneself. Cory was a truck driver. He had told me that when we met last week.

—How are things on the road?

—Aw. You know. Hey have you met my wife?

He turned to a large bottomed lady with a lot of make-up and a pierced nose. She was gossiping with another lady. She clearly did not want to be interrupted. She was really charming. She really was. She half-turned. Trying to conceal her annoyance and disgust. Fortunately the band started. Her eyes flickered at me for a half second and then both she and Cory turned away.

I don't blame them. I don't blame Cory. You see a lot of people when you're the greeter. You don't necessarily hit it off with all of them. I mean I don't care. But I'm not your fucking buddy.

9

Sheetrock. You know. It seems like it would be fun. Just toss the crowbar at it. Break it. Rip it. Tear it down. I have to admit that I've done some of that. Expressed some frustration. With a crowbar. Ripping out sheetrock. And it probably works. To release the frustration that is. As for the sheetrock there are better ways of removing it.

Probably the best way is to use the saw-z-all. First you cut vertically. Then horizontally. Then you carry the piece to the dumpster. After that you can use the saw to cut the screws and remove it from the stud. It is dusty though. And tedious. By the time you finish one room your frustration is gone and you're just bored.

Probably the best solution for the boredom is alcohol. There is no reason that you can't remove sheetrock while drinking.

It was early December and I was over at the Ewell house removing sheetrock. It was a Friday afternoon. Dusky outside. I was in my own world. I wasn't drunk. Not really. But buzzed. I'd opened a bottle of wine around 4p and was a glass or two into it.

By six it was pitch dark and I heard a knock at the door. It didn't make me happy. When I'm working and drinking wine I like to be left alone. Well. OK. I almost always like to be left alone—working and drinking don't have much to do with it.

Anyway. I went to the door. It was the escrow officer who had prepared and recorded my deed. His name was Cleve. Cleve Matheson. But. That was not obvious to me at first. It took me a minute to figure out what was going on.

—Hello John.

—Hey.

—I saw the light and wanted to stop by and talk to you about the deed

51

we did.

Honestly I was not drunk. But I'd had a glass of wine. I'd been alone for hours—removing sheetrock. I was standing in a half demolished house. I was looking out into an early winter darkness at a vaguely familiar man in a shirt and tie. My mind was spinning a little. When he mentioned our "deed" all I could think of was Hester Prynne. I knew that wasn't right. This was a modern American guy standing in front of me. He surely had never heard of Nathaniel Hawthorne. Much less Hester Prynne.

—OK. Yeah.

—My title guys were looking at it this week and they noticed a mistake.

—Oh.

—Some people are closing on the house next to you and we need to match their deed to yours.

—I see.

—What I need you to do is to sign this quit claim deed over to the developer who built their house.

—I'm sorry?

—When you bought this place there was a survey. There was no survey next door so they just used the old legal description.

—Uh-huh.

—Now the legal in their deed doesn't match the legal in your deed.

—I sounds like their problem not mine.

—Yeah. Well. Actually it is mostly my problem. My title guys are telling me I need to fix it.

—Why not fix it with the developer? I mean it sounds like he should sign a quit claim to me?

Cleve looked at me pleadingly.

—There is no actual property changing hands here. We just need to make sure the legal description matches. For that we need you to show that you agree to the description in the recent survey.

—OK. Well leave it with me. I'll take a look at it tomorrow.

—Actually. The closing is scheduled for tomorrow. We need you to sign a quit claim to the developer so that he has a clear title before he tries to close.

Did I mention the dollar store? Three blocks from my house. The city council approved it. Industry that. Jobs. Taxes.

Naturally they opened before Christmas. Black Friday. Green Monday. You know. The national holiday of trash. Gorge yourself on trash. It is on the calendar. Isn't it?

For the grand opening they inflated a big red—I don't know—ball? Sphere? I'm not kidding. On the sidewalk in front of the store. A large— 10 foot tall—vinyl inflatable something. Round. Hell. Don't make me describe it. I have no idea. What is it? Do you not notice it? People? Are you walking into that store? Past the big red inflated vinyl round 10-foot globe of. Globe of what? I am struggling to describe it. What is it? It almost looks like a fist. Like a boxing glove. Like an inflatable Everlast red boxing glove. But with no thumb. Just round.

Can you walk past that? And not wonder? What is going on? What is wrong with us? This serves to attract us to a place to buy cheap trash? When I drive past on the highway I feel compelled to stop? To enter the dollar store with the red bulb in front of it? The red bulb is making me feel like I will buy plastic trash for myself?

On my way to work I drove past the store. It was early. The store was not open. The light was dim. Dusky. The dusky light of early morning in the winter. I looked for the globe. It was deflated. Lying on the parking lot. Like a giant used condom.

It reminded me of Greg Brown. The songwriter: *I watched my country turn into a coast-to-coast strip mall and I cried out in a song: if we could do all that in thirty years, then please tell me you all—why does good change take so long?*

—How old are you?
Michelle looked at me.
We were eating fries at the Frosty Freeze. Christmas decorations were up. At the Frosty Freeze they had painted the windows. With. Well. Snowmen.
—You don't have to answer.
—I'll answer. Why do you ask?
—Just wondering.
—I'm old.
—Yeah.
—If I tell you I'm 32 can I retract it after we win our court case?
—Like Senora Olivares?
—Yeah. How did you know?
—Know what?
—That I was thinking of her?
—It's that time of the year. Didn't we meet her at a New Year's party?
—Yeah but she didn't lie about her age until well into Lent.
—Let's talk about it again next spring shall we?
—How old are you?
—Pushing 40.
—Uh-huh.
—I'm 36. Can I ask you something else?
—Yeah.
—Do you like men?
—What do you mean?

—I mean you're 32. You're attractive. You seem to be single. Do you have a boyfriend?

—I don't.

—How can this be?

—I've had a boyfriend.

—I would expect so. Why not now?

—I'm picky I guess.

—No. You're eating French fries at the Frosty Freeze with me. Picky you are not.

She laughed.

—OK. So I was dating this guy named Matt in grad school. Really smart guy. But controlling. Wanted to tell me what to wear. What to think. I had to get out.

—Where is he now? Matt.

—Oh. He's a post-doc. Still calls me. I don't want to go back.

She paused. Ate a fry.

—What about you?

—Me? Why am I 36 and single?

—Yeah?

—Because I'm an asshole?

She laughed.

—No.

—Yeah. Actually I am.

—What do you mean?

—I mean I'm a little bit short tempered and set in my ways. Not exactly a sensitive easy-going guy.

You might think that a house breaker would be an environmentalist. But I'm not. I hate environmentalists. Environmentalism is just another hypocritical religious movement in a country that has too many of them already.

I once went on an overnight kayaking trip with a friend of mine. He invited a bunch of other people and it turned into a pretty big group. A group of self-righteous greenies as it turned out.

I'll never forget pulling up to a small town gas pump on the way to the put in. We had four pick-up trucks and two trailers for eight or ten people. We bought probably 80 or 100 gallons of gasoline. On the other side of the island was a rough-neck filling up his company truck. Big one ton dually. Big guy. Wearing coveralls. He was dirty and tired looking.

Nobody said anything until we were back on the road. Then it was open season on the poor roughneck and everyone who ever knew him. He was stupid. He was dirty. He shopped at Walmart. He beat his wife. He voted for the Bush family mafia. He didn't own a Prius. He was what was wrong with America. And on and on.

At the boat ramp it continued. Oil companies: Bad. Gas companies: Bad. Refiners: Bad. Energy companies: Bad. Electricity: Bad (unless it was solar). Oil: Bad. Gas: Bad. Coal: Bad. Pipelines: Bad. Powerlines: Bad. Roads: Bad. And the people who had anything to do with anything were bad. Roughnecks: Evil. Rustabouts: Evil. Drillers: Evil. Truckers: Evil. Frackers: Double Evil. Executives: Evil. Managers: Evil. Motivated by greed. Every one of them. Ruining the world. Served no earthly good. Should be jailed. Should be executed. Summarily.

I'm not kidding.

The whole time this went on we were outfitting the kayaking trip. A wilderness trip. Just some non-consumer nature lovers in tune with the earth right? The entire trip outfitted in local hemp right? Wrong. We had a huge rubber raft as a support vehicle. (It was made of refined oil.) It was stuffed to the gills with expensive organic food. With imported wine. With drysuits wetsuits fleeces jackets and paddling pants. With tents chairs tables stoves propane canisters and lanterns. With cameras phones tablets GPSs and gopros. It was—in essence—a floating oil well lithium mine.

The typical American environmentalist sits atop a pyramid created by miners loggers and drillers. All the benefits the righteous enjoy—have you ever known a greenie not to be loaded down with the coolest and newest gear while he or she sips a micro-brew in Moab or Bend?—are provided by oil companies or strip miners. Yet they are "against" it. Against them. Hate them. Hate them with an intense vitriolic hatred. Hate them murderously.

Look at those magazines. There are all those magazines. I won't name them. They have a green editorial stance. They publish exposes of bad people. Frackers. Fucking frackers. Drillers. Bad. Bad bad people. Meanwhile. On the next page. Is a listing of the 30 best places for a winter get-away. For the cognoscenti. For those who know what is right and good. Tahiti. Aspen. Milan. Presumably the subscriber will walk to Tahiti because he or she objects to drillers.

I once watched a movie with a friend. It was ski porn. But it had a conscience. All the sliders were hippies at heart. Stop climate change man. We've got to do something man. But before we do: Watch me use this helicopter to shred 20,000 feet of vert in the Chugach today. The whole movie was like that. Two hours of jet fuel dressing on a green salad of self-righteousness. When it was over the audience cheered. Every one of them got up. Completely covered in refined petroleum. They walked to the parking lot. To the ten thousand ski rack equipped Audis for ten thousand people. Not one troubled face. Zoomed off throttle open. Stop climate change man.

For me it would be enjoyable to see the drillers and the miners go Galt.

They should. They should say. "Hey. F all y'all. We're going away for a year. Have fun." I would laugh. Those skiers would be dead before the year was up. Couldn't feed themselves; couldn't dress themselves. The pyramid from which they cast a haughty eye on all the filthy roughnecks supporting it would collapse.

But. Anyway. The kayaking group had a great time. Floating. Eating. Drinking. Carrying on. All of it brought to you by Standard Oil. The whole trip fueled by frackers. As for me. I spent most of the weekend alone. Part of it was my own fault: I avoided the scribes and Pharisees. But it also became obvious that I had—without regret or shame— purchased a head-lamp and the alkaline batteries to run it at Walmart: I'd plucked and eaten grain on the Sabbath. At the take-out I packed up and left. I've never seen any of them again. Fortunately.

10

For where envying and strife is, there is confusion and every evil work.

James

Late December is a good time for insulation. Removing it that is. You can do it in your jacket. In your Carhartt coat. Pull it out of the wall. Roll it in a ball. Cradle it. In your coat. Out to the dumpster. Back for more.

Actually you need a mask too. A mask to breathe through. Like the ones they wore during the SARS scare. Or Ebola. Well. Not really. Not strong enough. Not for Ebola. I hate to think about Ebola though. That is some scary shit. But. Let's not digress.

Insulation is a pain in the ass. Every little fiber in your throat. In your eyes. In the fabric of your clothing. Maybe winter is no better? Your clothes are full of it.

On the other hand. During the summer your sweat attracts it. Fiberglass in every pore.

Hey I'm not against insulation. It is a great thing. I stuff it into every corner of my attic. It saves me a lot of money. But pulling it strip by strip from an entire house is irritating.

Anyway. It was something to do. I had the week off. The office was closed. The week between Christmas and New Year's. My friend was gone. My only friend. Michelle. She'd gone to Minnesota to spend the holidays with her parents and sisters.

Before she left I took her out to dinner. We talked about paintings. About books.

—Did you see the story about the guy who bought a Maynard Dixon at the thrift shop?

—Recently? Where?

—Yeah. Here. It was in the Box Elder paper the other day. Some guy went into a junk shop and bought a framed painting for three dollars. Turns out it was a Dixon.

—Did the buyer know? Or was it an accidental purchase.

—I'm not sure.

—How great would that be?

—Yeah.

—I was at an art festival once and this guy—rinky dink pen and ink artist—was showing an oil painting in his booth. Claimed it was an Edgar Payne. Same thing. Said he found it at the thrift store.

—Was it? A Payne?

—I don't know. It could have been. One of those Arizona paintings. You know. Those Canyon de Chelly style paintings.

—Those are really nice.

—Yeah. He said there had been some spray paint on it. When he removed the spray paint he found the signature. Claimed it had been authenticated. I don't know. No reason for the guy to lie.

—What would you do if you found one like that? Sell it or keep it?

—I don't know. Probably it would depend on what it was worth. A million dollar painting? I'd sell it. I can't have a Rembrandt sitting around the house. A ten thousand dollar painting? I'd probably keep it. You?

—I don't know either. Keep it I guess. What are you going to do all week?

—For Christmas you mean?

—Yeah.

—I don't know. I've got stuff. Work. A project I'm working on. You know.

—You really are like Christmas. Joe Christmas.

—Joe Christmas?

—You don't know. I got you on this one?

—I guess so. What is it?

—Faulkner.

—Oh. My one failing.

—Failing?

—I don't know what is wrong with me. But I can't stand Faulkner.

—Oh my gosh.

—I know. Two Pulitzers. A Nobel. The Congressional Medal of Honor probably. Everything. I'm just missing something.

—I thought.

—You would think.

—Not Sound and Fury?

—No.

—Not As I Lay Dying?

—Nope.

—OK. But Light in August is a piece of cake.

—Maybe.

—You should. I'll give you my copy while I'm gone. Try it.

—Maybe.

—Joe Christmas. Read it for Joe. You'll like Joe.

I was playing a radio. Pop radio. You know. FM radio. Hit radio. Which. At that time of year is full of all those crappy Christmas albums. Everybody's got one. I'm not kidding. Not just the pop queens either. There is probably one by the Sex Pistols. The Ramones. Anyway. The pop radio news came on. The announcer announced shopping—most of America was shopping. I don't know. It was something like that. A survey had just come out—finding that most people wait until the last minute to do their holiday gift shopping. It turns out that Americans wait until the 11th hour to start shopping. (This is what serves for "news" on hit radio.) It got me thinking about the 11th hour. What is the eleventh hour? I know that people use it to describe something that is pretty nearly too late. But where did it come from? From Matthew? The vineyard owner goes out into the marketplace and finds laborers waiting there. It is the eleventh hour. *Please.* He implores them. *Come with me to my farm. Work for me today. I will pay you a full day's wage despite the hour.* But this wasn't a story about bad timing—about skin of your teeth timing. Not for these workers. This was good timing. Lucky timing. Spectacularly good timing in fact. All the pay for just a twelfth of the work. How does it end? What is the moral? *Friend, I do thee no wrong: didst not thou agree with me for a penny? Take that thine is, and go thy way: I will give unto this last, even as unto thee. Is it not lawful for me to do what I will with mine own? Is thine eye evil, because I am good? Ha. Funny. I like that: Is thine eye evil because I am good?* This story is about those who came in the first hour. How apropos. In a nation focused only on inequality. Which is just another word for envy. If Bill Gates can afford it I should have one too. How do you know about inequality if you're minding your own goddamned business? If I want to pay him more than I pay you what business is it of yours? Is your eye evil because I am good?

My thinking—fortunately—was interrupted by a metallic screech from next door. The new neighbors were moving in. I guess Cleve's deed was done. Har. It was a couple. They had a boat. Camper. A Rhino. A trailer. A truck. Diesel. Two ATVs. A Lexus sport ute. Holy shit.

The guy—the husband—was going in and out from the U-haul. I could see him over the fence. He could see me. I offered to help with the dryer.

He took me up on it. Jerry. Jerry. Handsome guy. Friendly. Really an OK guy. He really was.

—You renovating?

—Oh. You know.

—Cleve was saying we'd have nice neighbors.

—Yeah. Where you from?

—Salt Lake.

—Working down here?

—Residency.

—At the Health Center?

—Yeah. A couple years. Then we'll see.

—Want to stay in the area?

—Naw. My wife wants to move back to Salt Lake. Be near family.

—When do you start?

—Start what?

—I mean. At the hospital.

—Oh. I've got a week to get moved in. Then back at it.

—A little bit of a commute for you.

—Yeah. I'll have some long days. But my wife really wanted this house. New. You know. Nice. She just really wanted it. Got a really good deal on it too. Came down from two sixty. We only paid two ten.

—Yeah great.

He laughed.

—We're already three hundred grand in debt. We figured what's another two?

—Yeah.

—It'll take a few years to pay it all back. You know. But when my residency is over. Get into a practice. You know.

—Yeah.

We were in the house now. In the laundry room.

—Here. Let's just put it here. I'll hook it up later. C'mon. I'll show you the place.

It was everything you could want. I mean it was everything someone could want. I mean it was everything people evidently do want. A certain kind of showy luxury. Not ostentatious really. Just sort of large. Living large? I don't know. High ceilings recessed lighting fake nice touches. You know. Little alcoves of cultured stone or something. Places where you could put. What? Dried flowers? I mean you see these houses everywhere. They build them in the millions. It is on the tip of my tongue. But I can't really explain it. I don't know. Big butcher block islands. But the Corinthian columns on the four corners aren't real. I mean they aren't real supports. They are there to indicate something. Tasteful luxury? What? The front of the house will have a two story entryway. Maybe a story and a half. Maybe a vaulted arch to the entry way. With that fake stacked stone. I don't know what it is really. I mean I think you apply it in sheets. It isn't really stone. It is rough to the touch. But you put it on like sheetrock. You glue it up. Glue it to the particle board I guess. It is supposed to look like you built your house of stone. Sometimes those places will have a little dormer looking thing above the vaulted archway. It will have a window in it. But it isn't real. The dormer is built on top of the roof. Built out of particle board. No entrance to the house from the dormer. To the attic. No entrance at all. Just a little pyramid of particle board nailed to the roof before the shingles go on. Then a window put in it. Then the roof finished. It looks like a dormer. But it isn't. It isn't anything. It is a flourish. But fake. Anyway. Like I said. This is what everyone wants.

—Master bedroom down here. My wife really likes the big bathroom.

—Yeah.

—Two bedrooms on this side. Shared bath.

—Yeah.

—Great room.

—Wow.

—Kitchen.

Jerry's wife was in the kitchen. Putting dishes in the cupboards. Danielle.

—Sorry. I forgot your name.

—John.

—Hon. This is John.

She stuck out her hand. I shook it. I looked her in the eye. I didn't dare look down. She was very nice looking. Very well dressed. Nice hair. Nice make-up. Somewhat high heels. Well built. Amazingly. Well. Built. Almost a little too much better than average. No gravity at work on any of what was there. A low cut blouse. Like I said. I kept my eyes on hers. I did not look down.

—Nice to meet you.

—Likewise.

—John lives next door. He helped me move the dryer.

—Yeah. Actually I live two doors down. But I do own the place here. Next to you. I mean I own them both. I live in the one and I'm working on the other. I'm. You know. Working on it.

I was sort of rambling. Embarrassed. They were both looking at me. Barbie and Ken. Lord. It was time to go.

—Well. Let me know if you need anything else.

Jerry thanked me.

I turned. Passing a table. The kitchen table I guess. There was mail sitting on it. Catalogues. The top one. Clothing. Women's clothing. The picture was of a very attractive woman in a very slinky dress: Gravity was at work on the dress but not on the woman. Vixen it was called.

—You're welcome.

I went out.

It's a good story. It really is. A well woven plot. It is. And very little of that Joycean stream of consciousness crap. That is the stuff I really dislike. I shouldn't. I mean Joyce. He sits atop the pinnacle. Right?

Anyway. It was good timing. Reading about Joe Christmas. Not shopping. Not drinking egg nog. Not fiddling in the yard with a vinyl santa—inflatable vinyl santa. Not going to parties. No Christmas dinner. Nothing. I didn't even go to church. I worked a little on sheet rock. On insulation. On clean-up. Filling the dumpster. And reading. Reading about Joe the orphan; Joe the rebel; Joe the fornicator. Reading about Joe at the planning mill; Joe at the cabin; Joe in the jail.

Some of it was annoying. Stuff sort of like this: He was quite still. Implacable. And still. Not moving. Cold. Still. Unmoved. Unmoving. His eyes set. Stony. Nothing could be read there. There was nothing in his eyes. His stillness was like a thing apart. A thing all its own. He could see himself there. Still. Quiet. Cold. Quite still. Immovable. Implacable. A stillness not human. But somehow fitting. Fitting him. In his essence. His essence was of stillness.

—Holy crap.

I would shout it. To no one. To myself.

—Enough already.

Then I would move on. It was OK. I mean it isn't a bad story. It really isn't. I just don't like the verbose style. I prefer a minimalist approach. Lean and mean.

But it was full of questions too. Questions about race. About sex. About God. Good questions. Questions about good. About evil.

11

I was at the Ewell house on the day after Christmas. I wasn't very busy. I was bored. Doing some odds and ends. A little clean up. I was having trouble getting motivated. Sometimes you just don't feel like tackling a big project. It was too bad. I had all day. I could have really made some progress. Instead I was pulling a few nails and poking around with the broom.

I heard a truck outside. I leaned over and looked out a window. Kendall. I put down the broom and went to the door. I stood and looked out. The truck coughed to silence and the guy got out. Gave a shout.

—Hello!

—What are you doing?

—Saw your truck and thought I'd stop.

He came across the yard and up the stoop.

—C'mon in.

We passed into the living room. What used to be the living room. Our boots echoed on the floor.

—Well. Well. What you got going on here?

—Oh. You know. Just a project.

He laughed. Kendall. A burly guy. Rustic. Frayed and well-worn. But neat and clean. With a trimmed beard. And a lisp.

—A project like your last project?

—Yeah.

He laughed again. A friendly hearty laugh. In his mouth were a couple of broken teeth. He stuffed his hands deeper into the pocket of his threadbare chore coat. Clean. Neat. He was of uncertain age. Not young. Could have been 49. Could have been 71. Or anything in-between.

—How about you? What have you been doing? I haven't even seen you in—I don't know—six or eight months. You been around?

—Yeah. Got a little work up on the mountain with those new condos they're building. A little rough carpentry. You know.

—Well that sounds OK. You're a good carpenter.

—Aw. I get along alright.

Kendall was semi-unemployed and semi-retired. He worked as a handy man. Very handy. He was one of those guys who could do just about anything. And do it well. I'd hired him a few times to work on things around the house. The old house. The real house. The house I lived in. It was a ramshackle place with doors that didn't shut and floorboards that weren't flat. When I had a little extra money and something was really bugging me I'd call Kendall. He'd come and look. Go home and think about it. Then he'd come back and get it just right.

—You have a good Christmas?

—Yeah. The older boy came out from Vegas. Brought the family. Real nice time.

—He the one that works on diesels?

—Yeah. Diesel mechanic. Pretty good job. Hates Vegas though.

—Who wouldn't?

—I know. Huh? That wife he's got though. You know. She's one of those party people.

—Really? Your daughter-in-law? A partier?

—I don't know. She works at one of the casinos. Dresses real nice and wears all that make-up. Stays up late.

—Your kind of gal huh?

—Oh. We get along alright. She's nice to the wife and me. But I don't think she likes the small town life. The boy would like to move back. But she won't.

—How's your wife feeling?

—Doing better. She is up and around a little bit more. The doctor wants her to be out walking. We've been doing a little.

Kendall's wife had been through three or four back surgeries. She spent most of her time in the house. Kendall took care of her. Cheerfully. He never complained. Always had a good word about her. No resentment. In fact. Kendall had a good word about everything. A twinkle in his eye and a smile on his face. Always. I admired him. I really did. When he came to work for me I liked to hang around with him. Talk with him while he worked. He loved a joke. Easy going. Not goofy or lazy. But content. Content. Imagine that.

—Well. I better get back. One of the kids got a little bike and they wanted to get him riding it in the driveway.

—You don't want to miss that.

—No. Anyway. I wanted to let you know that I found those windows we were talking about last summer. The ones that might fit your old shed.

—Oh. Great.

—Yeah. I finally had the time to clean out my Mom's garage. I found those stashed in the rafters. They're in pretty good shape. I think they'll work for you.

—Sounds good. Let's try 'em. Whenever you've got time just go ahead.

—Yeah. It might be a couple of weeks. But I'll come over and see if they fit.

—Hey. And make sure you charge me for your time. I don't expect you to be doing it for free.

—If I can get it done I'll drop off a bill.

—OK. Thanks Kendall.

—Merry Christmas.

—You too.

A couple of days later I went back to work. The office was open again. On my commute I noticed a new house. Along the road. Near the office. It was sitting in what had been a hay field. Still was. A hay field I mean. Except for a tenth of an acre directly adjacent to the ditch. There was a new house there. I had not commuted for 11 days. Two weekends. Two holidays. Office closed for three more. Etc. Now in less than two weeks there was a house there. It came from Pennsylvania. From Michigan. From Texas. I don't know. The house came on a truck. In two pieces. A double wide. Siding joined. Roofing joined. On two dozen jacks. I could see them under the house. No skirting yet. Two new pick-up trucks parked in the mud outside. Big. New. Worth more than the house. Lights on inside. Living in it already? Yeah. There's the dish. Fucking TV.

Another half mile. I turned in. Parked. Used my code to open the door. It was mostly quiet. I like to get to work early. Get started before all the chit chat. I went to my office. Turned on the lights. Swung the door most of the way shut. Booted the computer. Sat. Leaned back. Looked at the wall. Thought about what I'd been doing two weeks ago. There was a light knock. The door swung open. Dustin.

—Hey.

—Have a good break?

—Yeah. You?

—Yeah. Spent the whole time thinking about taking a new job?

—Really? Where?

—Up in Montana. Old college friend up there. Has an opening. It's not guaranteed or anything. He just wanted me to think about it.

—Well? Why not? Is it a good situation?

—Yeah. It seems like it would be great. But I'm probably going to turn him down. Didn't really get an offer. But you know. Probably call him up later today and tell 'em that I'm not going to put in.

65

—Uh-huh.

—Not a good time to sell my house. Gotta wait for the market to move a little higher. I've got to make something on this one.

—Well. If it is a good situation you could just try to break even.

—I'm not doing that anymore. I did that on my last place. I paid $150,000. Put in a new chain link fence. New doors. New windows. Did it myself. Only out the cost of materials. But still. I lived there five years. When I was ready to move it took me ten months to sell the place. I got one fifty for it.

I didn't say anything. It sounded OK to me. I mean. He wasn't ahead. But he wasn't living under ground either. That is the thing. Everybody wants to make a killing. But a house is a place to live too. There is no such thing as free rent. It costs something to live anywhere. Dustin must have read my mind.

—Plus. I was paying $1,000 per month for my mortgage.

—Whew. That is a lot.

—Yeah. I had to borrow pretty much the full amount. Had no down payment. Hardly any equity when I was done either. I was paying interest only.

—Yeah.

—Figure $30,000 for the cost of materials for all the upgrades I did and it comes out to $1,500 per month. Basically like rent. I paid $1,500 a month in rent. And it wasn't much of a place. Hardly livable when we moved in. My first wife hated it. For fifteen hunnerd I should have been living well. Can you imagine what I could have rented for that? And then I coulda just walked away. Wouldn't have had to sell it.

—Yeah.

—So I'm not doing that again. Right now I need to get about three fifty.

—Wow.

—Yeah. I've really got to make a killing on this one. It is the only way to get ahead. Not going to do it from what I make here. Hey. I'm not complaining or anything. It is what it is. But you know what I mean. You've got to plan for the future. Figure out what you're going to need to maintain the lifestyle.

—Uh-huh. The lifestyle.

—Buddy of mine down in Arizona is doing it too. He's got it made though. Electrical contractor. Knows all the subs. He buys a place. Lives in it for a while. Gets these guys to come in and do all the upgrades. Squeezes 'em. You know. You wanna work with me on some other projects I got going on you gotta give me a good deal on this one. They do it too. Pretty soon he can sell it for a bundle and move to another place. Start over with the whole deal. Me? I can't do that. I've gotta do the work myself. You know what I mean. So. I'm not going to let this one go cheap. I gotta get my money out of it.

—Yeah.

—Besides. The wife. You know. She doesn't want to work our whole lives away. Living in crumby places. You know. She wants to travel. Maybe retire a little early. So. You know you've got to find some way to get ahead. And. Believe me. You're not going to do it from the ole nine to five.

Dustin was sitting. He had taken one of the chairs in my office. Ten minutes ago. He was evidently just warming up. He looked out the window a minute and then turned back. Started again.

—Now my oldest kid. He's got it figured out. I started on him young. Told him that he should be a doctor. That's where the money is. One doc I know—guy at my church—makes a million a year. And the respect. People don't argue with you if you're a doctor. You tell 'em what to do and they do it. My kid listened too. Got a scholarship. In college now. Doing good. Pre-med. Straight As. You know.

—Yeah? Good.

I was wondering how long this was going to go on. I was wondering if I needed to get up and offer to refill his coffee cup. To paraphrase Wallace Stegner. This guy had one mode of conversation: The monologue.

—I shoulda done it myself. I was pre-med too. But I dropped out. Not out of college but out of pre-med. It was tough. I was young. I was only 17 you know. I shoulda stuck with it. But all that organic chemistry. You know.

The office was waking up. Warming up. Filling up. A few people walked past the door. A couple of them waved. I waved back. Trying to distract Dustin. Betty stopped. Looked in. Front desk lady.

—Oh. There you are. I just sent a call back to your desk. Wright? Bill Wright?

—Oh. Crap. Yeah. I told him to call me here. Thanks.

Betty moved away. Dustin stood.

—Gotta talk to that guy. He is selling a real nice fifth-wheel. Camp trailer. You know. Trying to get him to give me a good deal.

He went out.

I turned to the computer. Opened the email. After almost two weeks it was clogged. Most of it wasn't useful or relevant but it was still going to take an hour to sort through it. Right away I noticed a string of messages between my boss and a database engineer from the other office. They were engaged in a lengthy misunderstanding. I started typing.

—Joe?

I looked up. It was Michelle.

—Welcome back.

—Thanks.

—How was the break?

—Good.

—When did you get in?

—Saturday night. I had the day—yesterday—to get over my jet lag.

—What is it? One hour? Two?

—One. I can't really complain. I'm on my way to Arshel's for a take-out coffee and donut. Sandy wants it. Come?

—Hell. Why not? I haven't been able to get anything done anyway?

—Sorry. I didn't mean to interrupt you.

—No. It's just. Don't worry about it. I'm happy to be interrupted by you.

—You are?

—Sure.

—What did you do?

—What do you mean? I didn't have any free time. You gave me an assignment.

I stood up and walked around the desk. I walked up to her. Her eyes were bright. She put her hand on my shoulder.

—I wasn't making you. I just thought you'd like it.

—It was OK. Better than The Sound and the Fury.

—Why?

—Oh. You know. All that stream of consciousness. I've admitted that I'm an intellectual failure. A real light weight. But I just can't make anything out of it. It gets better at the end. You know. Jason. When you get to Jason's point of view I can follow it. I'll grant you that Jason is an ugly bigot. But at least I can understand it.

We were in the parking lot now.

—My car is over here.

—I can drive if you want.

—No. This is my mission. For Sandy. I can drive.

She unlocked the door. Both doors. I got in. It was cramped. She offered to help me with the seat.

—I'm OK. It can't be more than two miles. How's the folks?

—Good.

—Good week?

—Yeah.

—Brother come?

—Yeah.

—Sister?

—Yeah. Everybody was home.

—Brother-in-law?

—Yeah. One big happy family.

Michelle had an older sister and a younger brother. The sister was a buyer for a regional retailer. Married. The brother-in-law was a lawyer. Somewhat arrogant. Not much appreciated by the family. The brother was a grad student. Something of a deadbeat from what I could tell. Going to graduate school because he could. And because he had nothing better to do.

—Dad happy with it?

—Oh. I don't know. He doesn't like to hang around much. Prefers to be out and about. At the hardware store. At the coffee shop. He volunteers at the county sheriff dispatch office. He likes to talk. Hang around with his cronies. Tell stories. Or lies.

—Your Mom? She happy with the week.

—Oh yeah. You know. You know how moms are with all the family around.

We got to Arshel's. A café. We went in. It was a mom and pop kind of place. Which was nice. The coffee was bad. The donuts greasy. We made a take-out order of four or five cups with half a dozen donuts. We waited.

—Did you work on your project?

—A little.

—What else?

—I went on a few hikes.

—What else?

—I did some reading.

—What else?

—Am I missing something? That is about it. Nothing very exciting.

—Did you call your parents?

—I did.

—Why don't you spend Christmas with them?

—Well. It's a long way.

—Every other year then?

The cardboard take-out tray arrived. Michelle paid. I picked it up. We went out. Back to the car. Squeezed in.

—Drive past the office. Let me show you something.

We drove in silence for a moment.

—Pull over here.

We were on the shoulder of the road. Directly across from the new house. Blue. The house was blue. Blue vinyl. On sale at the vinyl mine.

—Have you seen that before?

—What?

—That house.

—I don't know. I can't remember.

—You haven't.

69

—I haven't?
You haven't. It wasn't here last week.
—Oh.
—It is something I dislike.
—What?
—We can go back now.
Michelle u-turned and started back.
—I dislike cheap plastic houses. In hay fields.
—Oh.
—My parents?
—Yeah?
—They live in one.

12

In the town where I live the electrical grid is managed by the municipality itself. The guy who hooks you up to the power pole in the street is a city employee. It was time to disconnect the electricity so I called him.

—Shayne?

—Yeah.

—This is John over on seven hundred north.

—Hey John.

—I'm working on that house next to mine. You know. The blue one. The Ewells used to own it.

—I thought the bank had that one?

—Yeah. But I bought it out of foreclosure. Bankruptcy really.

—Hey. Good idea. If you can afford it. Get it cheap and make a killing when the market comes back.

—Yeah. Hey. Actually I'm going to tear it down. Am tearing it down.

—Oh. Yeah. OK. Going to sort of develop that property yourself huh?

—Yeah. Like that. Hey. I'm want to pull all the old wiring out of the house. Can you come and disconnect me?

—You wanna pull the meter and all that?

—Yeah.

—OK. Might not be today. But I'll be over as soon as I can.

—Thanks Shayne.

I ran 200 feet of extension cord from my shed. I put it in the window at the Ewell house. I wanted to be able to use my lights and tools.

When Shayne was done I went to work on the wiring. Romex. Is that what it is called? Anyway. I had to pry out the staples. But otherwise

71

removing it was easier than installing it. I didn't do any "pulling." When pulling was required I simply cut it. I threw the pieces in a pile in the middle of the room.

This was a money making job. Roberts at the recycling place would pay for this. Copper. I could probably get a buck a pound. More if I wanted to strip the insulation. I guess it is sometimes done by burning it. Burn the insulation off. Get more for the clean copper. Or with a utility knife. I tried that for a while. It's not impossible. Run the razor blade down the insulation. Peel it. Throw it away. Clean wire. But I soon stopped. It was too time consuming. Hey. I'm not above it. But I'd rather get the roof off. The foundation broken. The pumpkins in the ground.

Michelle followed me out of the staff meeting. It was the middle of January. The first staff meeting since before Christmas.
—Why do you always sit in the same chair?
—It is for the repetition.
—The repetition.
—Yeah. The events of the past are neutralized. The war—30 million dead—the dislocation, the loss. It is inconsequential.
—What are you talking about?
—I'll give you a hint. The main character has a last name that sounds like the game played with a ball and 12 pins. The author's last name is usually a first name—the first name in fact of the man who wrote Ozymandias.
—That's two.
—Two what?
—Two hints.
—I made it easy. Not that you need it.

The next morning. Early. I was working. Sitting in my office. She came in. No knock. Sat down. Looked at me. Shining eyes.
—I knew you'd get it.
She giggled.
—I googled it.
I thought for a minute.
—Vertical search? Or horizontal?
She started laughing.
—Horizontal.
—See. All Binx needed was the internet.
—Let's go to the movies.
I looked at my watch
—Now?
—No. Tonight. After work.

—I don't like going to the movies.

I paused.

—I do, however, enjoy going to old theatres and carving notches in the furniture.

She laughed again.

—I mean it though. We should go to the movies.

—Tell you what. Let's rent a movie.

—OK.

—Something Gregorish Peckerish.

She was laughing out loud.

—OK. That way we can do a horizontal search together.

She left my office. Laughing.

I sat and thought about her comment. Horizontal? Together? It seemed flirtatious. To say the least. But I wasn't sure. I never had succeeding in calling her bluff. I had asked her to do that thing with me on Thanksgiving. And we'd been friends ever since. But was there something more?

I was probably doing something wrong. I don't know. I never was very good at getting girls. When I was in college I remember being scolded by a house-mate. He was in a frat. Cool. He was cool. I mean he really was. Good looking. Confident. A hell of a guy. After a party at our house I remember him telling me.

—You coulda been making it here. Making it there. Making it everywhere.

I could have? Making what?

One nice thing about the internet age is that you don't have to go to a movie rental store. With a broadband connection and—sometimes—a couple of bucks you can watch any movie ever made. From the house from the office from the car.

That night we watched—what else?—To Kill a Mockingbird. We sat together on an old sofa in my living room. I was a little distracted. With her there. Not far from me. But the movie is engaging. It is a good movie. Maybe a little too good. Good for the self-righteous. Good for the liberal do-gooder. A little hard to swallow for those of us who are less than perfect. For those of us who are assholes. We recognize that we don't really live up to the standard of Atticus. But we're the only ones. All y'all are just like him. Stand up to the lynch mob and all that. Completely without bias or bigotry. Or. Like Binx says: *all of you believe in the uniqueness and dignity of the individual—even while hating his guts.* But I digress. It is quite a fine movie. It really is.

Afterwards we sat and talked about it. Michelle was turned to me on the sofa sitting with her legs crossed. Her knees were between us.

—The irony is that The Moviegoer was published before Peck even played Atticus.

—I can't remember.

—Yeah. Percy published in '60 or '61. The movie didn't come out until '62.

—OK. I'm having trouble remembering it all. It has been years since I've read Mockingbird. Let alone Walker Percy. I only picked up it up last night so that I could keep up with you.

—Better get going. After Moviegoer I'd recommend Lancelot. Another favorite. Love in the Ruins. You know.

I turned too. To face her. I leaned back against the arm rest. I pulled my knees up too. I was looking at her across two sets of knees. I kept talking.

—The only trouble with reading Walker Percy is that you want to put down the book and pick up a pen.

—Start writing yourself you mean?

—Yeah. You get carried away. You get to thinking that you can tell that story too.

—Which story?

—Well. You know. The story of Binx Bolling. The story of Mrs. Turpin. The story of Boo Radley. Jack Burden. I don't know.

—A line-up of southerners.

—A what?

—Southerners. All your examples are from southern writers.

—Suttree?

She laughed.

—See what I mean?

—OK. Sorry. I've only been to Alabama Mississippi Louisiana Tennessee once. Each. But the same is true when you get half way into Tender is the Night. Or Elmer Gantry. Or to prove I can go coast to coast Angle of Repose. I'll tell the story of Oliver Ward. OK. Not Elmer Gantry. I take back Elmer Gantry.

—Why?

—Because I'm not an atheist. You'd better be an atheist to write that one.

—So why don't you do it?

—Do what?

—Pick up the pen?

—Me?

—You.

—Yeah. Like I said. I get carried away.

13

In vain a zealous evangelist with a felt hat and flowing tie threads his
way through the crowd, crying without cease: 'God is great and good.
Come unto Him.' On the contrary, they all make haste toward some
trivial objective that seems of more immediate interest than God.

Albert Camus

The Ewell house had no air conditioning. Not even a swamp cooler.
Which was a surprise. Most cheap houses in the western United States are
built with a swamp cooler. A good way to handle the hot days. Until it
starts leaking. Which it will.

Anyway. Sometimes. During July. When the Ewells were there. I
would see a piece of particleboard in the bedroom window with a small AC
unit wedged beneath it. The windows were made of vinyl and they opened
by sliding sideways. Not the best configuration for an AC unit that need to
have the sash pull down on top of the sheet metal. The solution—one
solution—was to slide the window out of the way remove the screen install
the AC unit and fill the open space with a board. That was the Ewell's way
of doing it. And. Hell. It was OK with me. I mean. I'm not above it.
Looks kind of crappy. But what do I care? A lot of what I do is crappy
too.

In any case it saved me from needing to remove a central air
conditioning system. The Ewells took the window AC unit with them.
Leaving me to remove only the heating system.

There was a gas furnace in the attic with a cold air return directly
below—a grate in the ceiling of the dining room. There were grates or
registers in each room as well. These were in the ceiling too. This was
where the hot air came out. When the furnace was running air was sucked

from the dining room and heated. It was blown into each room through the duct work.

Have you ever lived in one of those houses? It is hot when the furnace is on—blowing warm dry air everywhere. It is cold as soon as the thing shuts off—all the heat going out through the cheap windows and doors. Warm and comfortable. Cold and drafty. Warm and comfortable. Cold and drafty.

Loud too. The furnace cuts on and wakes you up. Settles into a steady hum. You fall asleep. It gets too hot. You wake up. You throw off the blanket. Fall asleep. The furnace cuts off. Wake up. It is quiet. You fall asleep. It gets too cold. You wake up. Pull up the blanket. Fall asleep. The furnace cuts on. You get up. Stumble to the thermostat. Turn the furnace off. The house drops to 42 degrees. You go get your sleeping bag. You fall asleep. The alarm wakes you. You go to work with bags under your eyes. It's a good system.

With the exception of the furnace itself the rest of the heating system is easy to remove. There are cheap registers in the ceiling of each room and there is flexible duct work from the furnace to the registers. In the case of the Ewell house the installer hadn't even bothered to properly attach the flex duct. To remove it required only that I peel off some tape and drag the whole thing to the dumpster.

When everything else was done I lowered the furnace to the ground floor using a couple of ropes. I cleaned it up and sold it on Craigslist for $50. Pretty good money for a house breaker.

Speaking of money. These are the economics. On a good year I can bank up to $30,000 from my job. Extra. Over and above my expenses. I save about half my monthly pay plus any bonuses or raises. I don't know. Some years it is only twenty five or twenty eight grand. Maybe it seems like a lot to save. But my living expenses are low. I own my house so there is no mortgage. Same with the pick-up truck. No car payments. I do have to fork over for utilities. And fuel. But I heat with wood and I'm not an aggressive driver. I've got to buy food of course. And I admit to a weakness for good bread and good cheese. I shouldn't spend four or five dollars on a loaf of bread from Pierre's Bakery but sometimes I do. And wine. I don't mind a good Australian Shiraz. Otherwise I'm not extravagant. I don't care how I look. I mean I don't go around like a slob but I have no need for fancy clothes.

Anyway. After two or three years I might be able to save between fifty and ninety thousand dollars. My goal is to never pay more than one hundred grand for a house I'm going to break. With that as a target I can afford to buy a house every two to four years.

When I bought the Roundy house I probably overpaid. I got it for ninety but it was probably worth sixty or seventy. Heck. It was my first project. I was a rookie. Plus I had to deal with that realtor—Nate. It wasn't that Nate outsmarted me it was just that I couldn't get him on the phone. He didn't return calls and if I caught him by accident it was always a bad time. Because of this I could never tell what was going on with my offer. Well. On the other hand. Maybe Nate did outsmart me. I guess preforming like a dip-shit may have simply been a strategy. I probably should have called the bank. Acted ignorant. Worked my way up the phone tree. Got a manager on the line. Made like Hunter S. Thompson: Ah. Yeah. I'm calling about that house? No. Doesn't seem to be a realtor involved. Well. Yeah. There is a guy over there sometimes but he is visibly drunk and not wearing any pants. I consider him dangerous. Maybe a dealer in illegal drugs. For that reason I've been unable to approach him about my offer . . . without first firing my .357 magnum into the air as a warning.

Once the Roundy house was mine I could economize. And I did. I cut off all the utilities and sold the fridge and stove and dishwasher for a couple of hundred bucks. It lowered my purchase price—after closing costs—to $92,500. That is still a lot of money. But hopefully I won't have to pay that much again. With the cost of the dumpster and the earthwork plus some tools. Minus the money I made selling salvageable and recyclable material I probably spent an additional $2500 to break the Roundy house. An investment of $95,000 then.

Of course that doesn't include my time. Which I'm not going to do. I mean. This is a hobby. How many people sit around calculating what they should be earning while they relax at the fishing hole? I value my time. I really do. Probably more than most people. I don't have a TV for one thing. Fucking TV. But ask yourself: What would you do if you didn't have to work? The answer is something you'd be willing to do for free. If you'd enjoy doing it for free you don't bother calculating the value of the time spent doing it.

Currently the Roundy lot is worth probably $45,000. I know. It seems like a lot. But it is pretty big: .35 acre. And it has water. Irrigation water. Water for the yard and the trees. In the western United States water is a big deal. If you don't have water it is tough to have a garden. I mean. You can run your culinary water outdoors. But it is expensive and wasteful. Better to have irrigation water. The Roundy lot would probably be worth $30,000 without it.

So—to put it simply—I paid $95,000 for a piece of real property that is currently worth $45,000. I lost $50,000 on the deal. Or. I sunk $50,000 into a hobby. Let's see? Guy I know. Big snow machiner. He and his wife. He likes the Ski doo. She does too. What are they? Twelve or thirteen each. They got two. They haul them in an enclosed trailer. Ten thousand. Ten thousand dollar trailer. Safety? Avalanche bag beacon shovel probe. Let's say another three to outfit the couple. Clothes? Helmets? Backpacks? Gloves? Boots? I'm going to stop at $40,000. They've sunk $40,000 into a hobby. They get out on the mountain four or five times each winter. They make payments the rest of the year. I don't know. They probably enjoy life more than I do. But our long term costs are probably similar.

After a couple of good snowfalls I asked Michelle to go skiing. I drove my truck through six inches of fresh snow to the ford. It was frozen but the middle looked thin. I could see the dark water flowing below. I decided to park. There was no sense getting stuck.

Michelle was fit. Athletic. But not an experienced skier. She stalled on the thin ice. I cringed but she came over. We slugged up a small hill. I broke trail. We crossed a meadow. It was mostly cloudy. But now and then the sun shot a beam into the meadow.

We worked up another hill. When we got to the second meadow I made a loop. Back at the start I turned into the track. The going was easier now. The track was partly packed. We made another full lap. At the start again the track was in good shape. I stopped and waited. She came up.

—You ready for a fast one?

My question was interrupted by the sound of a motor. Back down the road. Near the ford. It came up. Revving. I listened for a minute. It faded. Then came back. Then faded. Someone goofing around. I turned. Michelle was close to me then. Rosy cheeked and smiling. Very nice. I looked away.

—Let's go. We can set a record on this one.

I went out. Kick push glide. Kick push glide. I made a lap in just two minutes. Michelle was further back. Maybe three. She came up smiling. Slightly winded but happy.

—Another?

—Of course.

After two more we got back on the road. In our climbing track. Heading down. The woods were quiet. When we got to the first meadow I could see tire tracks. In fact that was all I could see. Our ski track was gone. Shredded. Torn up. Why? You have the whole road. The whole mountain side. The whole wide world. But you have to trash my track? You have a motor. You could have gone anywhere you fat fuck. But you have to drive up my track. What? Are you fucking lonely? Don't want to be alone in the woods? Want to be close to someone?

Have you ever noticed this? People can't stand to be alone and don't want you to be either. See your shit got to come and fuck with it.

I didn't say anything. I mean. I can be an angry SOB. I really can. And

I sincerely prayed for that ATV rider to roll over and snap his neck—I prayed he would. But we'd been having a good outing. I wanted Michelle to want me. Women don't like angry men. Or. At least. They shouldn't.

The thing about going up to ski. About driving in the winter. Driving off the pavement. Driving your truck in the snow. With a girl. Is that you can get stuck. Sometimes you need to dig yourself a path to the road. To the oil. To the asphalt.

I remember getting high-centered one time. I was alone so no one had to be late for Thanksgiving dinner or anything. But it took me two or three hours to get out. The snow was crusty and I actually got on top of it. Driving on the surface. When the wheels broke through the truck was resting on the crust. None of the tires touched the ground. They were spinning in the sugary snow between the crust and the dirt. I had to lay down in the snow and thrust the shovel under the truck to break the crust. I dragged it out piece by piece.

Finally the truck settled and the wheels reached the ground. I got in and drove back and forth and back and forth in a little 15 foot patch until I had the whole thing compressed and compacted. From there I used the battering ram technique: Driving forward and breaking the crust until I lost traction and then backing up and doing it again.

But nothing is possible without a shovel. A shovel is your best friend in the woods in the winter. You can almost always get yourself out with a shovel. Unfortunately nobody carries one. I've almost lost count of the times I've found guys out in the woods. In the snow. In the winter. In the mud. Ice. Slop and slush. Usually stuck. Not one of them carrying a shovel. I usually help these guys. I mean. I'm not going to leave them out there.

One time I found a guy from Tucson. In a Volvo. Not far from the highway. Maybe half a mile. It was getting dark. He was stuck. Sitting in the car gunning it. Had been for an hour from what it looked like. The snow under his tires had been turned to ice. Wouldn't get out of the car. He had shoes on. Sneakers or something. And pants. So he wasn't exactly in the uniform. But he had no coat. No gloves. No boots. No shovel. I pulled up and asked if he wanted help. He did. I got out and used my shovel to dig him free. He watched me. I put my tow strap on him and bumped him. That was really all it took. From that point he was able to skitter back to the pavement. On his own. I followed.

He stopped to thank me. I guess he was excited. With relief. It made him talkative.

—Dude. I'd of been OK. I've got my survival gear.

I thought to myself: "Dude. If you carried a shovel you wouldn't need survival gear." It reminded me of Sergio Leone: You see, in this world there's two kinds of people, my friend, those who carry a shovel and those who are stuck in the woods.

Another time I was coming down the canyon in the snow. I could see that someone else had tried to come up after me. I watched their tracks. They were obviously struggling. In and out of the ditch and a lot of footprints. Finally I saw them. The young lady was on the road and the guy was driving . . . sort of. They were gangsters. Hats backwards hoodies tattoos cigarettes. They were also stuck. I pulled up and got out. They had a two-wheel drive sport ute (rear wheel) a little dog in a sweater and nothing else. No coats. No hats. No gloves. No boots. No shovels. Nothing. At least they—like Mr. Tucson—were wearing pants and shoes.

I offered to pull them out. They took me up on it. The guy pointed to his license plate. Louisiana.

—I've never driven in the snow.

—Uh huh.

I didn't necessarily need the explanation.

It took me a few minutes to get hooked up to them to pull them back onto the road and to make sure they could return to the pavement. During that time they talked a lot. They told me about how they had planned to move to out west. And so on. But by the end of the monologue they'd reached a conclusion.

—We're going back to Baton Rouge. We're not cut out for this.

Back in the truck I turned on the defroster. Michelle looked across at me. Picked up one of my gloves. It was an old leather work glove with duct tape across most of the fingers. She waved it at me.

—What is this?

—A glove.

—Why don't you get something without tape on the fingers.

—Actually I saw a nice pair at REI recently. But they were fifty bucks.

—That doesn't sound like too much for some ski gloves.

—On Amazon I can buy ten used books for that.

She laughed.

—What is on your list?

—All the King's Men. Blood Meridian. The Sheltering Sky. Stuff like that. You know.

She laughed again.

—Don't you want to think some more about it? You're the only guy I know who can rattle off a list of books that he wants to buy.

—Yeah. I know. I'm kind of a loser.

—I'm not saying that.

—I know you're not. But I recognize that I'm not exactly the life of the party.

—So what is the project?

—The what?

—The project?

—What do you mean?

—You went nowhere for Thanksgiving. You went nowhere for Christmas. What are you doing? Whenever I ask you say you've got a project. I've been to your house. I don't see any projects.

—Oh. Yeah.

—Is it illegal?

It was my turn to laugh.

—It isn't illegal. But it probably isn't normal either.

—You some kind of creep?

—Yeah. How does Lyle Lovett put it? *Son you can have my tooth of gold but do I really have to go?* Something like that.

—Or Radiohead.

—Yeah. Radiohead. No. Not creepy. Just unusual.

—Then what?

—Well. I'm taking down the house next to mine.

—Taking it down?

—Yeah.

—Why?

—I don't like it. It is an ugly soulless box. I don't want to look at it anymore. How is that?

—Is it yours? I mean do you own it?

—I do.

—How long have you had it?

—Oh. I don't know. Six months.

—You recently bought it.

—I bought it last fall.

—You bought it to tear it down?

—I did.

We were driving slowly down the mountain road. It was snow packed. The windshield was fogged. I was concentrating. I was carrying two shovels but didn't necessarily want to use them. Michelle said nothing for a while.

—Was it supposed to be a secret?

—No.

—Then why don't you ever talk about it?

—Because I want you to like me.

—What does that have to do with it?

—I don't know. It doesn't sound like the kind of thing an intelligent and attractive young woman would want to talk about.

—Can I see it?

—Yeah. I guess you can.

I decided to try a nicer church. You know one of those so called main line churches. Big parking lot. Traditional building. Lots of retired people.

It was fine. It really was. Everyone was nice and all. Friendly. At the passing of the peace they all said "nice to meet you." For the sermon there was a skit. Lots of laughter and clapping. I mean who could complain? I'm a positive person. I really am. I'm upbeat. I love that stuff. You can't really be too happy can you?

Or fatuous. Can you be too fatuous?

It wasn't bad. Really. I made it almost to the end. It wasn't so much the up-tempo jazz interlude as the weather. Honest. We'd had a cold winter rain and the foothills were laced with cloud. Fog. I went out and started the truck. I left the windows down so I could smell the bruised sage. The icy drizzle soaked through my shirt. I didn't use the throttle. I put the truck in gear and let it idle across the valley. It was a wet Sunday morning so I had the gravel to myself. The almost constant recreational traffic was absent. I thought about the skit: A guy who wanted to buy a Porsche. Was that God's will? I couldn't remember the answer. Honestly. I really think we should just leave him alone. God. I mean. Doesn't he get sick of it? Of American's praying about Porsches? I would. If I were him. For myself I stick with Dorothy Sayers' dictum: *Nor let God intervene unless the difficulty be worthy of his attention.*

14

Siding. This week it was the siding. Time for the blue plastic to go. Go into the dumpster. It was another one of those things you couldn't recycle. Mostly because it was too brittle. I don't know. Did the manufacturer expect it to last five years? Eight? Ten? Throw-away siding for throw-away houses.

Actually it wasn't bad everywhere. On the north side it was mostly intact and flexible. On the south side it was not. The sun does it. The sun damages it. The sun makes it brittle. It is ready to shatter. You grab a piece and it disintegrates in your hands. And all over the ground. It's a mess. You'll be picking up shards of blue plastic for years.

It's like those fences. You know the white plastic fences? Vinyl. Vinyl fences. Like a Kentucky horse farm? Rolling for miles over the green hills. Then the sun gets on the rails and they start to sag. They turn yellow. They break. They fall down. Then there is the silly McMansion. Six. Eight years old. Covered in vinyl. With a vinyl fence. The fence is shattering. A million pieces of white plastic rolling for miles over the green hills.

The thing about it is that it is easy. It is instant. The plastic comes out of the mold. Comes to your house. The installer installs it. Voila. You've got siding. You've got a fence. Instant fence. Instant Kentucky horse farm. No need for all that measuring. That cutting. That painting. That work. Instant horse farm. Installed by the installer. No work required. Even when it shatters in the sun. There is no work required because I can just step over it on the way from the car to the house.

Actually leaving it in the yard is better than what some people do. Some people collect it. Collect the old vinyl fence and put it in the truck. Then they drive out to the valley. Out to the public land. Out to where no one is looking. Off the main road. Up a little draw. In behind some pinyon.

Dump it. Big pile of sun rotted vinyl. Pretty soon a piece of it gets kicked into the trail. An ATV runs over it. It shatters. Then another. And another. And another. Like snow. Covering the ground. Every interstitial space. Between the sagebrush. Packed into the trail. A white vinyl fence. Shattered into a billion pieces. Covering the ground like snow. Except it never melts.

As for the Ewell siding I started on the south side. It was a lack of self-discipline. In February the south side is the nice side. We have relatively mild winters in Box Elder County but it is still nice to work in the sun.

Vinyl siding is a snap together system. It is supposed to be easy. Easy to install or repair. And I suppose it is. But it is especially easy to remove. Most of the pieces are floating. They are not nailed to the sheathing. They are supposed to expand or contract with the weather. Once you've unsnapped you can remove a lot of siding in a short time. It is a pretty easy job. Except for the brittleness. You have to be patient with brittle plastic. There is a lot of clean-up. I spent most of my time picking the shards off the ground. While I picked I wondered why vinyl siding was supposed to look like clapboards. I mean. Who thought of that? Vinyl siding could look like anything. Why try to make it look like wood? It doesn't look like wood. It just looks ugly. Where does it come from that something beautiful like an old clapboard sided house needs to be replicated for those who don't know and don't care? Why not make plastic look like plastic? I don't know. Siding could be shaped to look like a water bottle. What difference would it make?

Once the panels of siding were removed I had to go around and pry off the J-channels. Or whatever the plastic around the edge is called. The strips that the vinyl panels slide into. These were nailed. Not tightly. But it was a little extra work. And more breakage. But pretty soon all of that was in the dumpster too.

It was Friday. Friday the 13th. The 13th of February. I was sitting at my desk at 10a. I was reading a synopsis. One of our assistant editors thought this manuscript had potential. It was about Cotton Mather. Really. Cotton Mather. Not a bad topic really. Old Cotton. He was an interesting guy. But could we really sell a book about him? Who would be next? Jonathan Edwards? Of course. And why not?

Michelle came and stood in the door. It was something she did every day or two. She usually had something interesting to say. Today was no different.

—You know that scene from Grapes of Wrath when Rose and Connie are trying to do it quietly? In the back of the truck or something? Under a mattress or something?

—Yeah.

—I've been thinking about that.

I just looked at her. She was giving me an impish grin. Was she flirting? Was she suggesting something? I liked her. A lot. We were spending a lot of time together. We were friends. She'd told me that. But I was never sure what to make of her. Did she like me? Did she want something more? What was this business about the Rose of Sharon?

—Why?

—I guess it's because it's Valentine's Day.

—Tomorrow. Tomorrow is Valentine's Day.

—Yeah.

—By why are you thinking about that dead-beat Connie right before Valentine's Day? He was hardly a romantic leading character.

—I know.

She paused.

—So what are you doing for Valentine's Day?

—Hang on now. I don't want to be conflated with Connie.

—Even if I'm Rose?

There it was again. Was I being dense? Or was she suggesting that she'd like a furtive meeting with me under a mattress? I let it pass.

—I'd rather be Tom.

—OK. Tom. What are you doing for Valentine's Day?

—I don't know. You know. Driving to Tehachapi. I don't know. I've got projects.

—Projects. Well. Sandy wants to have a party. Sandy is having a party. A Valentine's Day party. At our place. Tomorrow evening. Seven pm. Wanna come?

—Well. I don't know. I guess so. You're going to be there?

—No. I'm inviting you to spend the evening with Sandy.

She rolled her eyes.

—OK. That sounds alright. But only if the Rose of Sharon is there too.

—I'll make sure of it.

There were eight or twelve people in the house. Mostly from Illium. It was OK. It was sort of a girl's party. Not really my kind of thing. But it was OK. There were some snacks. Lots of wine. I sort of hung around the kitchen island talking to one of the ladies who orders stuff for the company. You know. Copiers. Office furniture. Stuff like that. She's been around for a while. I sort of know her. We were just talking about stuff. You know complaining about work and that kind of thing. Or. I should say that she was talking. I was just hanging out.

—I mean she's nice and all. But I have to do her job for her.

—Yeah.

—She is constantly in and out. Kids sick. Gotta go to the doctor. Be in late. Can't get the car started. You know.

—Crisis every day?

—Yeah. She's like that. Totally self-centered. The world revolves around her.

—Yeah.

—Even when she is there she isn't paying attention. Constantly on the phone. Texting. You know.

—Yeah.

—Then she has to tell me all about it. Takes up my time. Doesn't care about me. It's always about her. Doesn't even ask how I'm doing.

—Yeah.

Michelle came through the kitchen. She had this guy with her. Dan. Dan Fulsom. Hell of a guy. Assistant IT something or other. Real smart. Real dickhead. Full of something alright. They were touring the house.

It made me kind of irritated. It really did. I hadn't come to this thing to listen to some lady complain about her boss. I came because Michelle invited me. Now here she was with Dan Full-of-Himself. Giving him the tour.

—It wouldn't be so bad if we were on the same pay scale or something. You know?

—Yeah.

—But here she is making the big bucks and I have to do everything for her.

—Yeah.

—I know she is looking for a new job. I just hope she finds something. Get rid of her.

Dan and Michelle came back in from the laundry room. They were smiling about something. I was pretty irritated. If I'd really been Tom Joad. Heck. I might have broken a board over his head or something.

—Taking the tour huh?

—You want one?

—Yeah. Right.

—You should. She gives a great tour.

Dan gave me a raunchy look. Michelle gave him playful push. Then looked at me.

—C'mon.

—I've seen it.

I was ready to go home. I really was. This wasn't for me. Michelle grabbed my arm and pulled me toward the laundry room. I followed and she let go. She walked through the laundry room with me following. She named it in a loud voice. She opened the door to the garage. It was dark. She stepped down. I reached to the light switch. It didn't work.

—That one is out.

—So where are you going?

—There is another switch near the door to the outside.

She walked carefully in front of Sandy's car. She crossed the garage to the man-door on the far side. I followed her. There was some light from the partly open door to the laundry room. It was behind us. Against the far door she stopped. She slid her hand up the wall to the light switch. The light didn't come on. I came up behind her. She turned to me in the half light. In one motion she stepped up to the threshold with her back against the door and pulled my pelvis against hers by grabbing my belt. I put one hand against the door to steady myself and one on the side of her neck with my thumb on her throat. I was a little surprised. I was even more surprised when my mouth met hers. Warm. Open. I took a breath.

—Was this what Dan was talking about?

—Talking maybe. But not doing.

My mouth met hers again. She licked my tongue. It felt good. Her hand had remained on my belt. She brought her other hand up and unbuckled it. Then the button and zipper on my jeans. I was more than surprised now. And a little anxious. And. Aroused. Without breaking the kiss her hands left my pants and went to her own. She unbuttoned and pulled down. Not far. Just enough that I could feel myself rising against her pubic bone. She grabbed the small of my back with both hands and began grinding herself against me. I was stunned. I was standing there with my hand on the door while she ground her womanhood against my manhood. I could hear the lady from the office furniture department. Her voice came through the laundry room and across the mostly dark garage.

—I swear. I don't know how people can live like that.

Michelle's kisses were hotter and stronger. The grinding continued. I was too excited. Suddenly her lips left mine and she gave a cry. I shushed her gently. She caught her breath. Her back arched. She was rigid. My face was against her neck.

When her breath returned and her back relaxed she was ready to talk. To whisper.

—That felt good.

—I'm glad.

—Can I help you?

—You already did.

She reached to the front of my shorts. They were soaked. Sticky.

—Oh. Happy Valentine's Day.

She laughed a little.

—Wanna get out of here?

—Leave the party?

—Yeah.

—I was just starting to enjoy it.

— You go out this door. I'll tell Sandy we're leaving. I'll meet you in front.

I hitched up my pants and went.

15

While thus employed, they were startled by a sight often so fearful in the waste and the wilderness, the print of a human foot.

Francis Parkman

As the weather warmed and we got into March it was time to let some air in. The Ewell house had just two exterior doors. I left those in place but went around the building removing windows. Vinyl windows. There were no windows in the bathrooms. There was one in the kitchen. There was one in each of three bedrooms. There were two in the "master" bedroom. There were two in the living room. Eight windows.

I'm of two minds about vinyl windows. On the one hand they are crumby looking and made of plastic. Sometimes they even come with strips of vinyl wedged between the layers of glass to make it appear as though there are individual panes. I hate that stuff. I absolutely abhor it when things are fake—molded of plastic—but someone tries to make them look real—hand crafted from wood. The designers of that stuff? May each and every one of them go to hell.

Manufactured windows are—on the other hand—incredibly easy to work with. The windows I have in my house—the old farmhouse—are hand-made. Bespoke. The wood shaped by a carpenter to fit a one-of-a-kind aperture. The craftsmanship is wonderful. Each piece of sash and sill carefully fitted; glass cut to the measure and lovingly glazed. I love the windows but they are certainly a pain in the ass. It is too easy to rot a sill or crack a pane. The next thing you know you are standing in your living room with the winter wind gently ruffling your hair. I've spent many an hour repairing and reglazing in the January sunshine—hoping to have it finished before nightfall. After all that I am easily tempted by the efficiency of a modern window in a modern house. It comes in a standard size. You take it out of the box. You put in in the hole. You tack it up with a couple of roofing nails. The glass is included. Sure there is some shimming and sealing involved but these things go quickly. The windows are installed in a day not a month.

Likewise the dis-installation. Once I got the hang of it—pealing back the flashing and pulling the roofing nails—the Ewell house went pretty quickly. With only eight to remove I could putter along for a couple of weekends making progress. I did some modest clean-up and put them in a small stack covered by a piece of tarp. I advertised them on Craigslist for five dollars apiece. It took a while but eventually a handy-man came out and offered me $30 for the stack. I told him that I wouldn't take anything less than $20. He laughed and gave me just that. I helped him load the windows into his van.

Once or twice—during the window project—Jerry stopped to talk. Jerry. My new neighbor. The doctor. Or medical student. Or whatever. He never said anything about the house. It was funny. He'd wander over to talk for 15 or 20 minutes. But. Here in front of him. A house being taken apart stick by stick. He never mentioned it. Never asked about it. Never said anything about it. Seemed strange. But maybe he didn't know what to say. Mostly he probably didn't notice it. Like nearly all Americans he had too much of himself in view to see anything else.

—My Dad was a personal financial advisor to some of those hedge fund guys. Southern Connecticut. Full of—like—billionaires. You know. Guys that worked at Goldman. Vice Presidents and such.

—Uh-huh.

—You know that part of the country? A lot of big houses. Nice cars.

—I've visited New Haven but that's about it.

—Yale. Yeah. My brother went to Yale. I was on the track team. Field. Discus. Throwing events. Hammer mainly. Got recruited by Colorado State. That's what brought me west.

—Oh yeah?

—I could've gone to Bates. Haverford. You know. Real good programs. Elite colleges. Ranked track and field teams. But CSU was the only Division One program that called.

—Uh-huh.

—Funny thing too. Coach called me out of the blue. Didn't even know who he was. I'm an east coast guy. You know. Fort Collins? Never heard of it. Anyway. It wasn't a full ride. But it was worth it.

—Yeah.

—College. You know. I really focused on the hammer. Freshman year.

Sophomore. A lot of personal bests. I was competitive. Got to where I had the school record in my sights. Junior year was going to be the breakout year. Then I hurt my back in a weight lifting accident over the summer. Couldn't practice that fall. Didn't have a good spring season. Kind of a bad deal. Never really got all my strength back.

—Oh. Uh-huh.

—Yeah. You ever throw the hammer? It isn't really so much about strength. It isn't always the strongest guys who are the best. It's all about the foot work. You know. Coordination and foot speed play a big role. Biggest role. Guys bigger than me I could beat them every week. It's all about your timing and speed. Lot of people don't know that.

—Yeah.

After the session at the Valentine's Day party I didn't have to wonder what was on Michelle's mind. I mean there were things about her that I still didn't understand. But I knew that she was flirting with me. More than flirting.

She started to come over to my house. Sometimes she would stay.

In the morning I'd make coffee. Bring it to her. She'd get up. Shirt and panties. She'd sit in my window with the coffee cup. She'd look at me. It was nice.

Well. She was nice. I wasn't.

After our ski outing I had brought Michelle to the Ewell house. The windows were still up. We walked through it together. Our voices echoing. She asked a few questions. Then. Nothing. We left the house. Neither of us had mentioned it again.

One Saturday morning I asked her.

—So what are you doing?

—What do you mean?

—Why are you hanging around with me?

—Because I like to.

—You do?

—I do.

—What about that business next door?

—What business?

—Don't play dumb. The house.

—What about the house? I don't care about the house.

—You don't care about the house?

—Why are you asking me about this? What did I do? I'm just sitting here. I don't care about the house.

—The house is stupid.

—What do you mean?

—The house is a waste of time and money. No one would do that to a house.

—OK.

—Don't you think?

—I don't know. I don't care.

—You don't care that I throw away tens of thousands of dollars? You don't care that I spend my time putting plastic siding in a dumpster? You don't care I am paying for that fucking developer to fill his truck with diesel?

My voice was loud.

—I don't know what you are talking about.

Her voice was quiet.

—You say that you like hanging around with me. Do you know what I am?

—What are you?

—An asshole.

My voice was definitely raised. I wasn't exactly shouting. But I didn't want to leave any doubt. I was angry. I really was. Angry at those fuckers. Every bit of space every lot growing cheat grass was just another place for a dollar store. Bulldoze it. Pave it. Even the cheat grass is gone now. The whole lot empty but for the styrofoam cups tumbling in the wind. None of that bothers anybody else; but it bothers me. And I wanted her to know.

—OK.

—It's OK that I'm an asshole?

—Yes.

What else could I say? I mean. I wanted to disabuse her of any notion that I might be a good guy. I'm not easy to get along with. I can have a sharp tongue sometimes. And I don't like trash. Or noise. My hobby—my business—is breaking houses. Dirty loud houses. It is stupid. It really is. It hardly seems fair to hide all that from someone who is sitting in your house in her panties.

On Sunday afternoon I drove up the frontage road. After 15 miles I turned up a two track. It was rough. I bounced along for another four or five miles. After a while it got muddy. I churned along looking for a place to park. I went through a little wash. On the way up the other side I got stuck. I backed up and engaged the four wheel drive. I spun a little more. I backed up again. I pulled forward. I could feel all four wheels digging deep. I crawled up out of the wash. At the next corner there was an opening in the brush—oak and juniper brush. I backed in and parked.

I got out with the camera and a water bottle. I drank half the water. I put the bottle back in the truck. I walked up the muddy road. After a quarter mile I noticed a cow or horse trail off to the right. I took it. It was less muddy but still a little crusty with snow and ice from a late winter storm. I started to notice that branches had been cut—head high—to keep the trail open. Horses then. The trail turned up a small canyon. In the shade there was more snow. But firm. The snow was hard and granular. Not too difficult for hiking. Kicking the boots in. It made me warm though. Kicking into the snow. Going uphill. I took off my sweatshirt. Tied it around my waist.

There were cat tracks. A big lion. Using the trail too. Why not? It must be easier than thrashing through the woodland. Even for a cat. But. What? Boot tracks? Yeah. I started to notice some old footprints. Several weeks old. Back when the snow was fresh. Somebody walked through here. Now that made me nervous. Mountain lions not at all. But people. Yeah. People scare me.

My father—who lives on the east coast in a double-wide—is always asking me whether I carry a side arm in the woods? In the canyons?

—What for?

—For the lions.

—The lions?

—Yeah. Guy I know. His brother-in-law went to Alaska. Or Canada. Somewhere. One of these hunting lodges. Wilderness lodges. You know. He was out hunting deer or elk. Moose. Something. Caribou. Anyway. He shot one and went to chase it. Got separated from his party. Skinned out the deer. Squatted down on the ground you know. All of a sudden something hits him in the back and knocks him flat. Big lion. Jumped him from behind. Good thing he was still wearing his pack. Claws went into the pack. Probably saved his life. Anyway the cat is biting clawing scratching yowling. You know. The guy pulls out a .357 and blasts the thing. Went a little ape shit. You know. Emptied the gun into the lion. It was lucky he was carrying it. My friend says his brother-in-law will never go anywhere without the gun. Wants to get a bigger one. .44 or something.

(When he said "ape shit" I started thinking about the time that Hunter S. Thompson tried to buy an ape in a casino bar in Las Vegas. The sale fell through after the ape bit some guy in the back of the head. The victim was not—evidently—wearing a back-pack. Well. Anyway. It might have been a hallucination. Thompson—according to Thompson—had been drinking tequila and eating mescaline for a week when he wrote that story. My Dad was sober though. And still on the phone.)

—Oh. Lucky.

—I'll say. I worry about you out there in the woods.

—Honestly. Dad. I'm as likely to be struck by lightning as attacked by a mountain lion. It's the people that worry me.

—Well. You never know. This guy wasn't expecting it either.

—Yeah. But he was up to his shoulders in deer guts.

—Lions. You know. They're getting to be more aggressive. Attacking lap dogs in peoples yards from what I hear.

Whoever had made the track was long gone—hadn't been there for two weeks or more. But I didn't like it. This is America. No one walks anywhere. Ever. Not in the west. The western United States is packed with ATVs. UTVs. Jeeps. Trucks. Motorcycles. Cars. Boats. Drones for god-sake. Nobody walks. In the past year I can count on one hand—one finger—the times I've been in the back country and encountered someone on foot. I'm not saying the back country is empty. It's not. It is full of people. Fat people. Full of fat people. But they don't walk: They squeeze the throttle or step on the pedal. On trail; off trail. It doesn't matter. Take me there by motor or leave me home.

So it makes me nervous to see footprints. If someone is walking around they are probably not normal. I mean. Look at me? I'm not well adjusted. I have no friends. And want none. I'm like Percy's Tom More. I love my fellowman hardly at all. And Tom More was—by his own admission—mad as a hatter. Of course. In contrast to Hunter Thomson. Tom More wasn't a real person. At least I don't think he was.

As I studied it I could tell that there were two tracks. Two sets of tracks. The same person. One set going and the other coming. Someone had hiked out and then turned around and hiked back. Nothing too strange about that I guess. But they went on and on. Again. It made me nervous. I know that some people might walk a tenth of a mile. Or. Sometimes half a mile if it says so in the guidebook. But I followed those tracks for two miles. Who would do that? Who would walk in the snow for two miles? Finally. I saw where they turned around. I relaxed. The snow was unbroken. I was alone. Except for the cat. Me and the cat.

Monday. I was at the office early. Trying to make some progress before all the typical meetings and interruptions. In came Dustin. Uninvited. Took a seat. Began. Apropos of nothing.

—You ever wonder where it all went?

—Which?

—All that money you made? What's your take home pay? I mean after taxes? You take home what? Thirty grand a year? Forty? Fifty if you're lucky. Working in a dump like this it can't be much. Let's say fifty to make it easy. Do you realize that you've taken home half a million dollars in the past ten years? I mean. Where did it all go?

I thought about a second soon-to-be-empty lot. I thought about two hundred thousand. I knew where that much of it was: In a dumpster. I wondered what to say. I needn't have wondered. Dustin wasn't there to hear my answer.

—You've got to think about this shit man. I'll tell you what. Getting divorced forces you to think about it. When I got divorced from my first wife I had to do it. If you're going to split your shit down the middle you gotta know what all shit you got. Know what I mean?

—Yeah.

—Shew man. Where does it all go? You look around and all you got is a bunch of payments. Nothing to show for it.

—Yeah. But in your case you've got a couple of great kids.

—Yeah. You spend it on the kids. Yeah. Making memories. I figure you're going to need to pay about eighty bucks a month for the cable. Maybe a hundred or a hundred and twenty if you want some of those premium channels. But the whole family can gather around to watch a favorite show or something. Everybody together on the couch. Yeah. You just spend it on living I guess. And a DVR. You gotta have one of those.

—Yeah.

—I never watch commercials anymore. I DVR everything.

—Uh huh.

—You see that new show they got on the History Channel?

—Naw. I don't really . . .

—Anyway they do a real nice job with that. Real high production values. I don't know how they can afford it. I just bought the first and second seasons for my Dad. He is retired now but he loves that stuff. They do a real nice job you know. Quality production.

16

My car broke down at the A&P three weeks ago and nobody would
come fix it so I abandoned it. Paradise is littered with the rusting
hulks of splendid Pontiacs, Olds, and Chryslers that developed vapor
locks and dead batteries and were abandoned. Nowadays people buy
cars, drive them until they break down, abandon them and buy
another.

Walker Percy

Festival of Homes. That's what they call it. Festival of Dopes. This
year's catch phrase was: Living the Dream. I'm not joking. And you pay.
Really. You pay. You pay for this shit. You pay to go look at obscenities.
The Parade of Homes. I think they call it that sometimes. You drive
around and pay to walk into some brand new luxury home. Fake. Fake
fucking luxury. You pay for this. You pay to look at this shit. Let me
clarify. If you want to take part in the festival of dopes you will pay to look
at fake luxury homes. They will be built by morons covered with tattoos.
Those morons will greet you heartily at the front door. They will have loan
officers nearby. There will be realtors available. With whom you may
speak. Like speaking with Socrates himself. Aristotle. Geniuses. It takes a
lot of knowledge to be a realtor. Not just any dumb shit can do it. No. If
you're a real dumb shit you'll have to be the builder. Or maybe you can be
the loan officer. Oh. Sorry. I forgot. These are not just builders. And
they don't build houses. These are "home builders." A job title made up
by people who think the rest of us can't figure out that a flatbed half-full of
2x4s and a few boxes of vinyl equals a goddamned house.

Anyway. In Box Elder County this year one of the builders was Chateau

Velocity. I mean that was the name of the company. Its claim to fame was that it built homes that were "magnificent." Really?! Let me guess? You build them at a high rate of speed too? I don't know. The brochure didn't mention that. But it did promise to make my dreams come true. Hum? My dreams?

But the reason I bring this up is that there was one in my neighborhood. A home. It was around Easter. Maybe the festival was scheduled for Easter this year. I don't know. But one of the stops on the tour—the parade the festival—was in my neighborhood. About two blocks from my house. From the Ewell house. I've been taking one down while he has been putting one up. Steve. Steve Young. The local builder. Big truck. Big arms. Tattoos. Very friendly. Knows a lot of loan officers. Parties with them.

I'd watched him build it. A piece of shit. Everything was fake. The hewn timbers above the front porch were made of Styrofoam—and spray painted. I don't know. I don't know what the stuff actually was. It wasn't wood. And I'd watched him spray paint them. The siding on the front of the place was glued onto the sheathing in squares. It came out of box. It was manufactured to look like stacked rock. For the festival these two features were called "rough timber beams" and "castle stone." It was a lie. The house was a lie. The timber and stone came in a box from a factory in China. It was a five bedroom six thousand square foot monstrosity. It had almost no windows and squatted in the dirt like a troll. The lot was small and there wasn't much left of it when the house was done but what remained had an instant lawn. About three days before the festival kicked off they rolled out the grass on a patch of sand out front and started watering. Beautiful.

And it was. Beautiful. Evidently. There were people in it all weekend. I drove by a couple of times and saw 'em waddling in and out. Drooling on themselves most likely. Morons. Morons just like him. The blurb for the place was full of descriptions of deep arches. Of columns. Of accents. But when it came to the fireplace the blurb used the term "true masonry." That says it all right there. For someone with eyes to see. Ears to hear.

That week my truck quit. I was at the bank. It wouldn't start. I mean I drove it there. It was working fine. I parked it shut it off and went into the bank. I came back out and it was dead. Battery? Couldn't be the battery. It was relatively new. Had been giving a good start all day and was only siting for five minutes. Bad connection? I got out the wrenches and pulled the terminals off the posts. They looked OK but I cleaned them anyway. And the posts. Grinding on them with a wire brush. Put it back together. Turned the key. Nothing. Starter? But wouldn't the starter tick or click or grind?

Hey. I like to think I can take care of myself. I like to think I can get the truck started in an emergency. But I fiddled with everything I could think of for 30 minutes. Fuses. Wires. Angle of the shift lever. Nothing. It was dead. I couldn't get it started. And really I'm not much of a mechanic. I can fix a flat and maybe install a new fuel filter but not a lot more than that. It is one of those things I don't enjoy and have never really gotten into.

So I opened the door. I put the key in and turned it to unlock the steering wheel. Leaning on the door post I pushed the truck back out of the parking space. In the parking lot I switched sides. Pushing on the steering wheel and window I moved the truck forward. Got it rolling down toward the street. My timing was good. There was no one coming. I jumped into the seat. We—the truck and I—had a little momentum now. We bumped across the gutter and into the travel lane. Carrying our momentum almost to the four-way stop. As we approached the stop sign I jumped out and started pushing again. I didn't stop. I rolled through. Swinging the truck to the left. Turning left. I was tiring quickly. I gave one last burst and jumped in. It was all downhill from that point. I was breathing hard and my legs were burning. I tried to calculate how many stop signs there would be. Four at least. The first cross street had a yield. I pumped the brakes a little but rolled through. There was no one there. The next one had a stop. I wasn't going to stop if I didn't have to. Clear again. Through. Another yield sign. Another stop sign. I was rolling OK. My luck was holding. On the next to last stop I had a close call. A conscientious driver would have stopped. But I wasn't conscientious. I was trying to keep rolling. I gave the other driver a friendly wave. She didn't respond. Just one more block. I could see it: Wayside Automotive. I rolled into the parking lot. I stopped a few feet from the garage door. Turned the key and got out. It was the end of the day. There was no one there but the owner. Allen. I went in.

—Well. It looks like you coasted all the way here.

I wasn't sure if he was joking.

—Yeah. It won't start. I was at the bank.

—Well.

—It's been running fine. Battery is relatively new. The lights work. It can't be that. But when I turn the key there is nothing. I came out of the bank and that was it.

—Probly the starter.

—But it didn't buzz or burn or anything. It worked like normal 20 minutes ago and now it doesn't?

—Yeah. They can do that. Sometimes you can tell that they're about to go but sometimes they just quit.

—Any chance you can look at it?

—I should be able to do it tomorrow.

—That's great. Not too busy?

—Naw. We've got some jobs. But no emergencies. Things have been a little slow.

—I'm surprised. It seems like you've always got somebody parked out front.

—Yeah. We're doing OK. But there isn't as much as you'd expect. People don't fix cars anymore. They just get a new ones.

He sounded like Tom More: Nowadays people buy cars drive them until they break down abandon them and buy another. I didn't mention it though. Not Tom More.

—Yeah.

—Everybody's gotta have new.

—I don't know. It doesn't seem very affordable.

—Tell me about it. That truck of yours. A four wheeler. If you wanted to buy one of those new. You're talking thirty grand. Forty. Depends on what you get. Hell. You can spend fifty or sixty.

—But if I spent that I'd have to live in it. That is about what I paid for my house. I'm not sure where people get the money?

—Oh. They borrow it. They make some big payments. Guys I know are paying $500 per month just for the loan. Forget about the insurance and fuel. Every month. You can fix a lot of starters for that.

I laughed.

—I'll check in with you tomorrow.

I walked home. It was a few blocks. A truck rumbled up from behind. I ignored it. I always ignore those bastards. Gunning it through the neighborhood. Might as well be at the Indy. The truck was directly behind me. I kept walking. Somebody shouted. I thought I recognized the voice. I turned. Kendall. He put the truck in park. Halfway in the street. Turned it off.

—What are you doing now?

—Oh. Walking home. My Chevy quit.

—Well get in. I'll give you a ride.

It was only a couple of blocks. But I climbed up. Kendall's truck was 40 years old. Beat all to hell. But clean. Neat. All his tools in a row. It started right up. He gave a big smile.

—I just got out of the hospital.

—You what?

—Yeah. Yesterday. In for a week.

—A week. What is going on?

—Oh. Hell. I had a perforated intestine. Bad deal. They weren't sure if I was going to make it.

—What caused it?

—Diverticulitis.

—What is that?

—Some kind of growth in the intestine. I wasn't feeling too good. I'll tell you what. I guess it kind of swelled up and burst. Then I felt really bad. All that shit leaking around inside.

—It sounds horrible. What did you do?

—My wife you know she can't get around. I need to help her. I thought it was something I ate. I kept plugging away. After a day or two my buddy from across the street stopped by. Lucky too.

—He saw something was wrong?

—Yeah. By then I guess I was white as a sheet. Infected. Bloated. He called the ambulance. Probably wouldn't have made it another day.

—Holy crap. But what about your wife?

—The boy came up from Vegas to take care of things. He had to get a week off of work. I feel bad about that.

We were parked in front of my house. I was looking at him. Shaking my head. He was a little pale. Seemed thinner.

—Are you supposed to be out here driving around 24 hours later?

He laughed. Winced. Reached for his abdomen.

—Ouch. Naw. I'm supposed to be home in bed. I'm doing OK. The wife wanted some bread for sandwiches. I made a quick run to the store.

—Hell. Kendall. I'll go to the store for you. What else do you need?

—Oh. We're doing OK now.

He looked straight at me. His eyes were twinkling.

—You better get out though. My wife is going to call search and rescue if I'm not home in five minutes.

I laughed.

—You didn't have to give me a ride you old goat.

I jumped out.

—I'm going to come over to your house in a couple of days to make sure you've got what you need.

—Aw. We're doing good.

I swear I'm not one of those people who quits attending a perfectly good church just because there is a skit about a Porsche. I'm not. I'm trying to learn to be patient. I don't fly off the handle. That is immature.

After a week or two—once Easter was out of the way—I went back to the nice church. The big main-line church. I mean. There was nothing wrong with it. Nothing.

This time the scripture lesson was from Deuteronomy. Chapter 30. Moses was dying. Moses made clear to his followers the choice that they faced. *See, I have set before thee this day life and good, and death and evil.*

I thought about it. Here it is. This is going to be a home run. No minister could fail to hit this one out of the park. This is the choice that all of us face. Every day. Life and death. Good and evil. Why is it so difficult to choose life? Why is it that I'd rather do what I want to do than what I know is right? What would the answer be? I set myself for it.

The pastor started with a joke. St. Peter. That is OK. All of us enjoy the St. Peter joke. Then a platitude about helping others—tutoring at the elementary school. Then a challenge to lose some weight. A joke about a little boy in Sunday School—it sounds like a squirrel but I know the answer is supposed to be "Jesus." An admonition to learn from the book of Proverbs. Finally he got into a long description of Twinkies. I'm not kidding. He was getting some laughs. Commenting about the texture of Twinkies. The nutritional value. I think he worked it all the way around to chastising us for preferring spiritual Twinkies over the hard work of—I don't know—tutoring at the school. But by then I'd quit paying attention. I perked up just once more when I noticed that he was coming to the punch line. Something about not settling for white bread when you can have the bread of life.

I found it ironic. Talk about white bread. That was a white bread sermon if I ever heard one—a real Twinkie.

On Sunday evening I had the newspaper. I was on the bed. I had one leg thrown over Michelle. She was reading a book.

—Oh. Lord.

—What?

—Wednesday. Wednesday is Technojet Day. The Mayor has signed a proclamation.

—It's what?

—Technojet Day. They're breaking ground on a new facility at the airport. Bringing jobs. Mayor is falling all over himself. Declared a new holiday.

—Wednesday is May First.

—Yeah.

—May Day.

—Yeah.

—I wonder what Lenin thinks?

I laughed.

—About Technojet?

Michelle laughed. She closed her book.

—It's funny. About four or five months ago some guy in church was negotiating a lease for an aircraft manufacturer. During the sermon.

—Must have worked out for him.

—Yeah. Too bad.

—It's getting late. I should go.

Yeah you should.

I rolled over and threw my arm across her breasts. I put my lips on her chin. She turned her mouth to me. After a minute I let her go and pushed her off the bed. She gathered her book and I followed her to the door. We walked down the steps to the yard. I kissed her again at the car door. She drove away. In the distance I could hear the whine of the highway. I went back in and looked at the Technojet article. The Mayor was hosting the Governor for the ground-breaking on Wednesday. And there would be a TV actor on the podium with them. Big draw I guess. TV actor. Fucking TV.

17

The Ewells used to have a lawn. Such as it was. Kentucky bluegrass. Crabgrass. Bermuda grass. Cheat grass. They'd water it sporadically and mow when the mower would start. By the middle of the summer it would be mostly browned out and patchy. But in the spring it would bounce back: Turn green and grow like crazy.

Anyway. It was my grass now. And it was spring. April. Best time of the year for grass I guess. A little bit cool and damp. I interrupted my work on the house to manage the grass. Some of it I mowed. Some I mulched. Some I sprayed. With round-up.

I love round-up. And I hate grass. Oh. I don't know. Maybe hate is too strong. But this is the semi-arid American west. Not really the place for rolling acres of emerald lawn. So mostly I try to get rid of it. Dig it up. Cover it up. Kill it.

You see what those developers do? They just make the dirt smooth install a sprinkler system—culinary water too—and roll it out in strips. Instant lawn. Set the timer. Hire someone to mow. And there you go. You're an English lord.

Time to build a house. A spec house. A plastic house. Fake. Got the property. It's got a few trees on it. An old orchard. A native box elder. Some weeds. Maybe a couple clumps of sagebrush. A juniper—made to withstand drought. A struggling pinyon. Survivors. Fuck 'em. Fuck the survivors: You start with the saw. Cut it all down. Then a dozer. A back hoe. I don't know. A big machine. A big yellow machine. Dig it. Rip it out. Get the roots. Bulldoze it. Plow it up into a pile. Burn the pile.

When the piece of crap plastic house is finished you run a matrix of PVC around the property with a pop-up sprinkler every six feet. Everything else is scraped flat. Scraped clean. In comes the yard. The lawn. The turf. On a truck. On a flatbed from suburban Provo. From Bakersfield. I don't know. It comes in rolls. You apply it. Like carpet. Like wall paper. Or rather. Your Mexicans do. You're the general contractor. You drive. That's what you do. You drive a big truck. Rat-a-rat-a-rat-a. You don't bend your back under the hot sun. That's what your Mexicans are for. In goes the lawn. It takes a single afternoon. Bingo. Uniform. Perfect. Plastic like the siding. Oh I don't mean that. Sure. It is alive. It will grow. With enough water. That is what the PVC is for. The sprinklers. Put 'em on a timer. Get the whole thing timed to come on for six hours per day. Preferably between 1000 and 1600. Insta-lawn. No care required. Except for mowing. But there are Mexicans for that too. Right?

Sell the house to some up-and-comer. Not a tree in sight. But. By Gawd. A lawn. A square of perfect turf. Sprinkled to green perfection every day. Trees are still there though. They are still on the site. They've changed their form. But they are still there. As charcoal. Under the turf.

After the Ewell family moved out I expected the bank to try to sell the house. A bank. Any bank. But nothing happened. For a couple of months. Finally I went to the county recorder's office. I looked up the property. It was owned by Amy and Aaron Johnston. Joint tenants. Who the hell? I thought about it. The Ewell lady. Her first name was Amy. Her husband was Rick. Rick and Amy Ewell. Let's say that Amy was the right woman. Then who was Aaron?

I went to see the building inspector-code enforcer for the city. Clive. Clive Morrison. Clive was one of those guys. Knew everything. Had been in every house and on every lot in the county one time or another. Fearless. Stuck his nose in if he wanted to. But respected. Everybody knew him. Knew what he was up to. Trusted him. He was honest. Tough but honest. Knew the code. Knew the ordinance. But didn't write you up just because he could. He wore a hunting jacket. Smoked a lot of cigarettes. His face was tan. Deeply lined. Permanent squint.

—Yeah. I know the place.

—Know who owns it?

—Now let me think.

—The deed says Amy and Aaron Johnston. The people who were living there were named Ewell.

—Yeah. That's right. Her second husband. Or third maybe.

—Who was it before? Do you know?

Clive looked at the sky. He was standing with his legs spread. Wearing work boots. Jeans. Hat from the IFA. Hands in the pockets. He took a long drag. Exhaled.

—Aaron something. Aaron Johnson

—Johnston?

—That's it. Aaron Johnston. Aaron and Amy Johnston. He worked over to the jail. Maintenance guy.

—Where did he go?

—Died.

—Died? He's dead?

—Yeah. Kind of a bad deal. Out hunting on the ATV. By himself you know. It rolled over and tore him up bad. Internal you know. Couldn't see anything. Sort of bled to death before they could help him.

—Awful.

—Shook some people up around here. I'll tell you. His Mom works at the little grocery out by the sawmill. She wasn't doing too good for a while. Really loved the guy.

—Of course.

—The wife. The gal there. Amy.

—Yeah.

—She was from California. Her Mom. Her Mom bought that house. Interesting lady. To say the least. Wanted to sort of get out of California. Decided to come out here and buy a house. Sight unseen kind of deal. Bought that place for two hundred grand or something. Paid cash.

—You've got to be kidding?

—Naw. That was during the boom years. Everybody was over-paying. Figured the value would go up forever. Anyway. She never really liked it. Paid some interior decorator silly money to get it all fixed up. Came out to live. Stayed a few weeks. Went back to California. Gave the house to her daughter.

—Amazing.

—Daughter moved from California. Got a part time job at the clinic. Stayed. Ended up marrying Aaron. When he died she went back to California for a while. Pretty soon that other guy was hanging around. Then he moved in. They had a couple kids I think.

—OK. It all makes sense to me but the bankruptcy.

—Bankruptcy?

—Yeah. Amy and Rick have filed for bankruptcy.

—Hm.

—Why file for bankruptcy when you own the house outright and you have a rich Mom in California?

—Good question. But I did hear somewhere that the Mom died too. I don't remember who told me. But. Yeah. She died too. In California somewhere. Died broke. That's what I heard.

We started to develop some habits. Saturday morning coffee was one of them. We'd meet early. Seven thirty or eight. At a dive café about half way between our respective homes. We'd each have a cup or two of bad coffee.

Poured from the Bunn carafe. We'd split a sweet roll. We'd sit there for an hour. Ninety minutes. Then we'd go. Separately. I'd go to work on the house. Or I'd cut some wood. Or I'd go out to the canyon.

—So you refuse to visit your parents?

—What? Who said that?

—Well. That day after Christmas. When you showed me the new house. You said that you hated your parent's house.

—I remember saying that I hated that type of house. I'm not sure I would say that I hate my parent's house.

—Oh. But you won't visit it.

—I will visit it. I don't hate it. I don't hate them. But. You know. We don't have much in common. Not much to say. *We quarreled so much it wore itself out.*

—What is that from?

—Arms. A Farewell to Arms.

—Did you grow up there?

—In that house?

—Yeah.

—No. We had a crumby old place. New England. You know. Hand hewn. Post and beam. Large old rooms. Drafty and cold.

—But they moved?

—Pretty recently. They sold the old place. Bought a piece of land. It was—in fact—a farm field. It really was. They had a double wide dragged in. Paved a driveway to the back door. Voila.

—Why?

—Why did they move?

—Yeah.

—They wanted the convenience. Everything new. No repairs. No maintenance. Push a button and the thing turns on. I can understand it. I really can. Maintaining the old family manse can be a big job.

—But you still resent them?

—Not resent really. Like I said we simply don't have a lot in common. They grew up in the late thirties. Early forties. Fifties. Post war. Really the boom years. You know. TV. Modern advertising. Everybody had a new Chevy. Tail fins. New music on the radio. They absorbed every bit of it. Ate Wonder Bread. Drank Tang. Traded in the car every year. They were true consumers. Still are. The fridge gives a shudder? Dump it. Buy a new one. You know.

—But you lived in a big old hand-built house.

—Yeah.

I laughed.

—Everything but the house. It was a financial thing I guess. They never could afford to sell it and upgrade. But my Dad really hated it. I remember him talking about it all the time. What he really wanted was an automatic garage door. With a heated driveway. No shoveling. No getting out to put the car away. All that stuff.

—We had one.

—What?

—An automatic garage door. Except we never used it. We never opened it. It stayed closed all the time because our garage was used for storage.

—Yeah.

—At one point my parents bought a new dining room set. They had nothing to do with the old set. It was perfectly good. So they moved it out there. Temporarily. But pretty soon they were stacking boxes of Halloween decorations on it.

—Still?

—Yeah. I mean it is all still there. Ten years later. Everyone parks in the driveway. The garage is too full of furniture to fit a car.

The waitress came back. We both took a refill.

—But your parents did some things right too.

—They did.

—Yeah. They gave you your love of reading.

—No. Not really. I was a reader because there was no one to talk to. My parents were busy. They weren't good listeners anyway. So I spent my time reading.

—I'm surprised. I figured that the whole family was engaged with books.

—Actually my Mom has always been something of a reader. But mostly pop fiction. Romance. Suspense. Best sellers.

—Not a lot of Camus for her huh?

—What about Babbitt?

—Babbitt? Where did that come from? Are you changing subjects?

—I am. Do you like it? It ought to be your bible. Right? I mean you can hardly make realtors seem worse than Sinclair Lewis does.

—You ought to provide verbal clues when changing subjects. And I do like it. It has some brilliant descriptions. Like the style of the Babbitt house. The fake fireplace. Or. I don't know. Maybe the fireplace was real. But it was unused. The family had an up-to-date modern furnace. But there was the fireplace. For effect. For style. Lewis calls it unsoftened by downy ashes and sooty brick. The fireplace comes with tools—andirons—like samples in a shop. Unused and unwanted items of commerce. Something like that. Great description. But overall it is difficult to like.

—What?

—The book. The character. The whole thing. I mean. I appreciate Lewis's sharp eye and sarcastic commentary. And he was a great writer. I mean he was extremely skilled. But he was so hateful. You almost end up feeling sorry for his characters. He creates these people—Babbitt especially—who are so awful. So pathetic. So ugly. That no one could love them like them or even tolerate them. The caricatures are so extreme that I almost have to stop reading.

—Yeah.

—You know what I mean?

—Yeah. Babbitt is greedy and self-centered. Babbitt is an ignoramus. Babbitt is an ostentatious show-off. Babbitt is a self-indulgent glutton. Babbitt is a fool. Babbitt is lazy uncultured and silly.

—Of course. And all the regular people—the empty headed regular people—can think only what they are told to think by the advertisers and by the vile Republican politicians and by the hypocritical protestant ministers. No one—save presumably the superior and prescient socialists like Lewis and H.G. Wells—can see that the whole thing is an evil conspiracy cooked up in smoke filled back rooms to keep the laboring man in his place.

—Lewis obviously hated business people—business owners. So he writes a book with a business owner so hateful that no one else can help hating business owners either. It is more like a piece of propaganda than a real story.

—The only time poor George seems human is when he sends his wife to the sister-in-law and has an affair. Only when George Babbitt is cheating on his wife and drinking too much does Lewis relent and make him seem semi-likable.

—It's because he becomes a liberal. That's why.

—Oh. Yeah. He is briefly a liberal. A friend of Seneca Doane.

18

Woe unto them that join house to house, that lay field to field, till there be no place, that they may be placed alone in the midst of the earth.

Isaiah

The windows and doors were gone. But it was time to see some more daylight. I went to work on the sheathing. Sheathing. Particle board sheathing. Particle board. Wood chips glued together and covering the frame. Screwed briefly to the framing.

Heck. Even having particle board was something. I know there are builders who don't bother with it. You put the sheetrock on the inside the siding on the outside and fill the gap with a little insulation. I've always wondered about burglars. I mean it seems easy. Right? Why bother locking the doors? With a pocket knife you peel away the plastic siding. You push the insulation to the side. You knock a small hole in the sheet rock. You're in. Family diamonds.

I spent a couple weeks on it. Not because it was particularly difficult or time consuming. But because it was boring. I wasn't motivated to work on it. I love this life. The life of the house breaker. There is nothing more exhilarating than seeing the last wall hit the dirt. There is nothing better than sitting in the middle of an empty lot. Maybe some pumpkins. But no plastic. Like any pursuit though there are days when it is hard to get excited. There are days when you have to force yourself to pull nails or remove screws. There are days when it takes a little self-discipline to get up and go clean up someone else's mess.

Anyway. I hit a lull during the summer. It was hot. I was pulling the sheathing. I didn't feel like it anymore. I felt more like sitting in the house. My house. With a book. I pushed myself to spend a couple of hours per week on it. Early in the morning or late in the day when the sun was less strong.

Most of the particle board came off whole. I stacked it to sell. More salvage. Some of it came off twisted or shattered. I threw it in the dumpster.

Anyway. When you're taking down the exterior sheathing you don't have a lot of privacy. What I mean is that people can see you. People driving by on the street can see what you're doing. Not that it matters. It's your house. You can break it if you want to. But some people think you're weird. Like the developer. Steve. Steve Young. Young Homes. Local builder. He built the house next door. Among others. Built it quick. Built it cheap. Fake luxury. Drives a massive truck. Is very tan. Has big arms. Is covered with tattoos.

On this day he stopped. Got out. Came and stood on the foundation. Very hearty personality. Very.

—Hey Buddy.

—Hi Steve.

—Whatcha doin?

—Oh you know. Just taking down some walls.

He laughed loudly and gave me a knowing look. Like we were in on something together. I never had liked him very much. In fact. I hated his guts. Wouldn't help him if I saw him pulled down by a pack of feral dogs in my front yard. Would cheer for the dogs.

—Whatcha going to do with the lot?

—Oh I don't know. Grow trees?

He laughed again.

—I know what you mean. It's nice to have a little garden.

He had no idea what I meant. To him a garden was just a place to squeeze in another piece of shit plastic mansion.

—Well. If you need anything let me know.

—Thanks Steve.

Steve jumped in his truck with a hearty wave. Hearty. What a guy. A real prince. He gunned his truck and left me in a cloud of diesel exhaust.

Right then I sort of felt like crap. I mean why? My vision of the world is of equal value to his. Right? Why does he make me feel inferior? I'm the stupid sod taking down a wall while guys like him—douchbags really— are gunning it around in monster trucks putting 'em up faster than I can imagine.

And trees. I told him I was planting trees. The thing about Steve. And trees. Steve Young. The developer. And trees. Any trees. But especially

crumby native trees. The box elder—noticed by Escalante. The pinyon—
one needle or two. The juniper known since Fremont as cedar. Or maybe
old orchard trees. Carried by—who was it?—the Bishop? The archbishop?
Cather's archbishop? Across the prairie. A cutting from France. Made it
across the wide Missouri. Down the trail. Santa Fe Trail. Oregon Trail.
Mormon Trail. Some trail. To the southwest. There it is. On the
property. The thing about Steve. And trees. Is this: He will absolutely rip
the shit out of them.

I was sitting at my desk. Michelle came to the door. She came at least
once a day. Looked in. Smiled. Said something.
　Today she was drinking water from a paper cup. She had a question.
　—If you're 36 why don't you have any gray hair?
　I just looked at her. She was like this. Unpredictable. In a good way.
Not flighty. Flakey. Weird. But fun. Always thinking of something.
Mostly something I couldn't follow. Like now.
　—I don't know. Living right I guess.
　—I'm starting to get some gray hair.
　—Um. OK.
　—It's not fair. I'm dating an older guy. But I'm getting gray hair and he
isn't.
　—Who are you dating?
　She rolled her eyes.
　—What made you think of this?
　—I don't know. Do you think I look old?
　She looked great. She really did. She almost always did. She had a skirt
a blouse. Plain. But nice. And those bright eyes.
　—Yeah. You look old.
　—So what is your secret?
　I sat there for a minute. I looked at her. I started in a hushed voice.
　—In my attic.
　I paused. Still looking at her.
　—I have a painting. A portrait. Of myself.
　She laughed. She threw the empty water cup at me. She swung my
office door. When she reached me she pulled her skirt to her waist so she
could straddle me. She got on the chair with me and put her face against
mine. Her eyes were shining.
　—You know why I like you?
　—No. Why?
　—Because you read.
　—Lots of guys read.
　She gave me a deep kiss.
　—Not like you.

I was starting to feel nervous. It was the middle of the work day. The walls were thin. Fortunately she lowered her voice.

—Can I see your attic after work?

—Yeah.

She kissed me again and pushed back. She stood up.

—See you later.

—See you.

—Dorian.

Then solar energy came to the valley. Taxpayer subsidized. It was great. Caused a bunch of distant urban environmentalists—which is just another fundamentalist religion—to have wet dreams. Especially because it wasn't in their back yard. They didn't have to look at it. Actually the power company came first. The regular power company. Implicated in dirty coal. My My. Built a massive substation. Where once had been sagebrush and a view of the mountains and larks calling on spring afternoons. But. It's OK. Isn't it? It makes us feel so good. So righteous. Pure. Sinless. Alternative energy. We built the substation on a huge weed free pad encompassed by razor wire. It was a religious duty. We are believers in the religion of alternative energy. Let us pray.

After the substation was finished there was something of a reprieve. But pretty soon—next door to the substation—there were temporary offices and big signs announcing the arrival of solar. The temporary offices did not have potties. Evidently. So they needed porta-johns. A whole block of them. Shantytown of sani-johns. The Hooverville of plastic potties.

They moved in during the winter. The roads were gravel and native dirt. So of course it was muddy. Right away the county road crew was out there paving. Hauling in more gravel to build a platform on top of the muck. Then chip sealing it. But hey. That is why we pay taxes. Right? At least our taxes are going to something good: We're paving the way to lower emissions. Hey. I ought to sell that to big solar. Big subsidized solar. Big subsidized solar slogan: Paving the way to lower emissions.

Solar installations require space. They require land. Acres and acres and acres of land. Hundreds of acres. Maybe a thousand. It must have been some farmer. I don't blame him. Really I don't. He probably got a good offer. A great offer. He could afford to get out of farming. Retire to Phoenix. Go live in a blue vinyl box in a good neighborhood with a pair of dollar stores. Instant lawn. Something.

Solar installations require fences. They required barb topped prison style fences. Miles and miles of fences. I don't blame them. Really I don't. Solar power is bad enough without having somebody monkeying with it. I don't mean that. God forgive me. There is nothing bad about solar power.

The back hoes arrived. The track hoes. The earth movers. The dump trucks. The water trucks. The tractors. You can't have vegetation at a solar power plant. Sagebrush? No. Rabbitbrush? Ah. Nope. Snakeweed? No. Not even cheat? Not even cheat. You've got to rip it all out. Pile the stems for burning. Leave the mud behind.

How about meadowlarks? Fuck no.

The county commissioners were ecstatic. Jobs. Soltec Solar was hiring 350 construction workers. Eleven dollars an hour. Minimum. Fifty hour weeks. I'm a rain maker. A job maker. Vote for me. Never mind that the job is gone in five months. I'm sorry son. How does Springsteen put it? Son don't you understand? You think they're going to hire you to run the thing? All you can do is drive the dozer. Once the dozer work is done you are too. Once the shit is ripped out of that meadow you can go back to the sofa.

They had a big poster hanging from the new fence. Soltec did. A logo thing. A motto on it. SOLAR EQUALS JOBS. Or some lame thing. There were two men on the poster. On the logo. Not really men but stylized outlines of men. They were engineers. Holding blueprints. I'm not kidding. They were muscular. They were looking into the distance. Holding up the blueprints. The men on the poster worked for Mao. Stalin. Not really. Not thirty million dead. Fifty million. I'm sure not. It only reminded me of that. And only me. Or maybe me and Binx. Where are you Binx? Can we sit in the same seat for this movie? The same one we sat in last time? No one else in the valley recognized the forms and figures of state propaganda. And why would they? They were driving dozers for $11 per day. I mean. Per hour.

The worst part of it was the off-the-grid guy. Kind of a hippy guy. And his wife. Had five acres of sagebrush. Had it for ten or fifteen years. On the county road. Sure. There was some occasional traffic. People going out hunting or camping. Getting a load of firewood. But not much else. Gravel. Quiet most of the time. Built an off grid kind of place. A little rustic. Home-made solar. Small wind. That kind of thing. Cabin of stucco. I don't know. Of clay and wattles made. A couple of goats. A hand dug root cellar. I never stopped to talk. Saw him a few times. Graying beard. Lean. Feeding the chickens. But decent. Decent and clean. Not trashy. Just really committed to making his own way.

BAM. How did that feel hippy? BIG SOLAR. SUBSIDIZED SOLAR. Our razor wire fence shining in the sun. Where once was a ragged semi-settled three hundred acres of farm is now a solar power plant. Hippies like solar. Right? I don't know. Like I said I never stopped to talk to the poor bastard. Even less now. Right there in front of him. In front of the hand-built house. Dozer ripping through the sagebrush. Loaders. Trucks full of pipe. Hey. They aren't trespassing. What can he say? Gone is the smell of bruised earth after a hard summer rain. Gone the silence of a winter morning. Gone the view to the mountain across the valley. Gone the coyote in the dark. Gone the call of the lark. OK. Not gone entirely. Those things can creep back around the edges. Especially the coyotes. But the peace. The quiet home-built sense of a place. Gone. Now it is simply pinched by another development. Solar development. Who knows? Maybe they'll get a dollar store.

I probably shouldn't feel sorry for him. He is probably one of those statist do-gooders. Always plumping for regulatory intervention. Use taxpayer money to force unaffordable ideas down the throats of the average guy who just wants to be left alone. Or maybe not. Maybe he is like me. Looking for a little elbow room. A couple acres away from the trash and the noise. A place to think. Who knows?

—Do you ever read non-fiction?

—I have a job in non-fiction.

—I know. But for fun. Do you ever read non-fiction for fun?

We were laying on my sofa. Partially dressed. Michelle had followed me home from work. She had been eager to get together. Her eagerness had been contagious. We'd left her skirt and shirt at the door. She was looking up at me now. Asking questions.

—Yeah.

—Like what?

—Um. I don't know. I really like Hunter S. Thompson. Although that may be partially fiction too.

She laughed. I continued.

—I like John McPhee. I don't know. Biographies. I like Stephen Ambrose. David McCullough. Why? What about you?

—I do. Very much. History.

—Yeah. Good. Like what?

—How about Bernard DeVoto?

—How about him?

—Across the Wide Missouri.

—Too long.

—I know. But I really like it. Year of Decision and Course of Empire too.

—A glutton for punishment.

—Tell me about it. Do you know Parkman?

—Not really. I might have read the volume on La Salle.

—Another good one. Although—like Thompson—there are those who might question whether some of it is fiction. Bancroft? Bandelier? Paul Horgan?

—No. Wow. You're way ahead of me.

I looked at her with appreciation. Ran a hand down her flank. She went on.

—Horgan wrote a biography of Bishop Lamy.

—Lamy?

—Yeah. From Santa Fe. You know.

—Um.

—Willa Cather.

—Oh. Cather's archbishop?

—Yeah. That's the one.

—I was just thinking about him the other day.

—Have you read Horgan's version?

—I haven't.

—I'll loan it to you.

—See.

—See what?

—That is why I like you.

—Why?

—Because you read.

—Lots of girls read.

—Not like you.

19

God don't lie. No, said the judge. He does not. And these are his words. He held up a chunk of rock. He speaks in stones and trees, the bones of things.

Cormac McCarthy

The builders. They get their sheathing on a flatbed. A semi. It comes in stacks. From the factory. Unload it with a fork lift. Or backhoe. Something. They need a lot of it. There is a lot of it on a house. The roof under the shingles is sheathing. Particle board. All the exterior walls under the vinyl are sheathing. A big house. Aren't they all now? Big I mean. A big house needs a lot of sheathing. Even the Ewell house—which was not much more than a box—had a lot of sheathing.

I had no plan for what to do with all of it. So I stacked it in front. By the street. Stacks. I made stacks. Not all of it. Some of it broke. The corners snapped off when I dropped it from the roof. I cut some of it in half. Made a pile of halves. Threw the broken sides away.

I put a FOR SALE sign on one of the stacks. After a while a guy stopped. Mexican. Beat up truck. Worse than mine. Dirty white t-shirt and jeans. Broken English. He pointed at a stack.

—How much? The wood?

—How many pieces are in the stack or how much does it cost?

—Cost?

—A buck a sheet. One dollar. Dollar each.

He nodded. Counted his way down the stack. There were 20 sheets. He pulled a $20 bill out of the front of his jeans. Handed it to me.

—Gonna try to get it on the truck?

—No. Trailer.

—You got a trailer?

—Yes. Come back later.

—OK.

He got in the truck and drove away. I watched him. I felt happy. I was happy to see that guy. Guys like that make me happy. Mostly I don't like anyone but I liked that guy. Friendly. Polite. Hard working. Goddamn. Those Mexican guys can work.

Reversing the war. 1846. Bunch of Americans. Good fighters. Went down and took California from the Mexicans. Took New Mexico. Arizona. Nevada. Utah. Good fighters. Americans were good fighters. Are. Are good fighters. (We proved that to our great sorrow the next time around.) But we won the war. That war. The Mexican-American War.

Americans took Utah. Took Nevada. Took Arizona from Mexico by fighting; Mexico is taking it all back by working. I'm not joking. Everything we have. We Americans. Will be owned by Mexicans soon. They're going to work us out of it. And it won't bother me a bit. They deserve it.

I went back up on the roof to remove a some more sheathing. But not for long. Right away the old truck was back. With a dilapidated trailer. I went over to help. But it wasn't necessary. Out of the truck came two or three people. Shouting. Whistling. Backing the driver. He put it in park and came out smiling. The four of them got after it and had the trailer loaded in minutes.

A young man came over. Perfect English.

—You selling the rest of it?

—Sure. Need it?

—Yeah. We'll probably be back tomorrow.

—You can have it all if you can use it. Hell. You can just take it for free if you've got a use for it.

He looked slightly embarrassed.

—No. No. We can pay.

—Building something?

—My father raises goats. We're putting together a barn and feed shed.

—Well. Like I said. I'm glad if somebody can use it.

The father came up. Smiling. Shook my hand.

—We'll see you tomorrow.

—See you tomorrow.

When June came we planned a hike. We went out on a Saturday. We went to the river. There were six or eight cars at the ramp. Subarus. New. Bumper-sticker environmentalists. Live simply. Stop Exxon. Live with a Subaru full of gear. Made of plastic. Made of oil. Made of material mined pounded boiled refined shipped spilled wasted. Drive out here on Exxon's back. Cheap fuel. Exxon didn't provide that did they? Put your hypalon on the river. Coolers. New fleeces for sitting around the campfire. Made of plastic. Refined oil. Complain of corporate greed. Not us. We're above all that. We buy local. We grow a tuft of hair under our lip. Our other car is a Prius. Battery of nickel. Grows on trees. Nickel. Doesn't it? Renewable. In fact. Better buy another one. Why not two. Priuses? Priuii? Yeah. True righteousness. Get a fleet of 'em. It's all renewable. Nickel. Doesn't require another mine. You just pick it from the organic nickel farm. But I digress.

We launched the canoe. Upstream. We paddled against the current. Not easy. Not hard. Just steady. You have to keep at it. We went up a mile. Two. A little more. It took an hour or so. We stopped at a small beach. We got out the sausage. The cheese. The chairs. We had a snack. We listened to the river. The afternoon was clear. Sunny. Warming.

—Ready for a hike?

—OK.

—It's a bit of a slog.

—OK.

—But worth it.

—Let me put on some shorts.

—Better leave the jeans.

—What about the long sleeves?

—You may want those too. It might be brushy.

We went further upstream. On a faint path. It was rough. But not far. We came to a small creek. A confluence. I turned to the right. Up the creek. I walked in the water now. It wasn't deep. Hardly over the sole of my boot. Or on the rocks. I was a little hunched. The walking was OK but the channel was overhung with water birch. Maple. Dogwood. Willow. I stopped after ten minutes. Looked back. Michelle was there. I waited.

—OK?

—OK.

I went on. Steepening a little. Going up. Small cascades. The light dim from the overhanging branches. The walls narrowing. It wasn't hot but I started to sweat. The climb. The humidity. A clump of wild rose. Scratching. A downed log. Go over. Another 15 minutes. 20. A branch whipped my cheek. No sound but the tinkle of water. Occasional shafts of sunlight into the gorge.

I stopped again. She came up. Sweating too.

—What do you think?

—Beautiful. How far?

—I don't know. Shouldn't be too bad. We've come half way.

Up again. Thrashing a little. Slipping on logs. Crouching under maple leaves. Feeling damp. Sticky from the humidity. More boulders. Cascades. Very steep. Up the creek bed. Slippery. Topping out. Waiting. Now together.

We were standing at the edge of a large clear pool. It was surrounded on three sides by the thick woods. On the fourth was a vertical limestone wall. Cracked. Down the wall trickled the stream in a 40 foot cascade. Cascade in slow motion. The fall broken by hanging gardens. The pool was partially open to the sun. It slanted into the clearing created by the pool itself. The air was still. The only sound made by the spray and drizzle of water. Down the wall flowing into the pool and out again.

I took off my shirt.

—Let's swim.

—It'll be cold.

—No.

I pulled her to me. I unbuttoned her shirt. She helped me get it off. Sticking a little from sweat. I bent and kissed her neck. Pushed my nose under her throat.

—Oh.

Her hands went to my shoulders. To the back of my head. I reached down. I unbuttoned her jeans. I hooked my thumbs in them catching her panties too. I knelt. Pulling them with me. Kneeling I untied her boot. I turned my face to her.

—Don't. I'm sweaty.

—I don't care.

I untied the other boot. Pulled it off. The sock. Pants. Stood. Pulled her against me. Kissed her face. Unhooked her bra. Dropped it on the clothes. Turned her. Pushed her to the pool.

—Go ahead. I'll be right behind you.

—It will be cold.

—No.

She took a couple of slow steps forward. Up to her knees. Looked back. Smiling. I had my pants down. Working on my boots.

—It's cold.

—Naw.

I followed her into the pool. She was waiting. Her back to me. Thigh deep. It was cold. I came up behind her. Wrapped my arms around her chest. Kissed her neck.

—It's cold.

—I told you.

She laughed.

—C'mon. Quick. Dive under. It'll feel good.

I pushed her.

She jumped back.

—No.

I went past her. Deeper. I got to the deepest point in the pool. Water to my rib cage. Cold. Icy. It was hard to catch a breath. I ducked down. Water over my head. Shock. Up. Gasping. Blowing.

—Whew. Your turn.

—OK. OK. Don't splash me.

—I won't. Come here.

She came. I held her. Rubbed against her.

—I know how to warm you up. Hurry.

She went down. Barely under. Up. Squealing. Laughing. Spraying. Flipping her hair. Turing to the bank. Quickly. I followed. Ankle deep she stopped. I came up. Face to face. My hands on her breasts. Nipples hard. I kissed her neck. Her mouth.

—Oh.

She said.

—Warm me up.

We dressed quietly.

—How did you find this place?

—It's not the only one.

—What do you mean?

—There is something interesting up every one of these creeks.

—You know them all?

—Most of them.

—How?

—I like to look around. You know. Just go for a hike or something. At least. I used to.

—Not now?

—Not as much?

—Why?

—Now I break houses. I guess I'm growing up.

By then I had my eye on another one. It was about half a block away. On the other side of the street. A corner lot. With a small brick house. The house was old and somewhat dilapidated. Not my typical target. I mean. I don't mind those older ramshackle places. In fact. I live in one. They're OK. Uncomfortable sometimes. But usually solid. And quiet. You can sit—after the vomit-like carpet is gone—on a hardwood floor in a back room and not hear the street.

No. The ones I want to remove are the newer ones. The bland plastic soulless boxes. Built one upon the other. Street upon street of empty sameness. Fake flourishes and cultured stone. How was it that Wallace

Stegner described the change? The change from places with character—individual character—made by a man's hand to characterless cities full of interchangeable blobs made by an extrusion machine? *A set used over and over . . ., a stroboscopic image pulsing to reassure us by subliminal tricks that though we are nowhere, we are at home.*

In any case I was interested in that house on the corner. Interested in maybe adding it to my business empire. Interested in buying it. Putting my money in someone's pocket. Someone who didn't care about the place—ramshackle and trashy. Another wise investment on my part. Taking tens of thousands of my own money and giving it to some pig who can't be bothered to pick the beer cans off the stoop. Leaving me with a place to clean up. On which I will pay taxes for the privilege.

Actually. I might not break that place. I mean. I might clean it up. Make some simple renovations. And keep it. Keep it for a guest house. Guests. Visitors. Those coming to Box Elder County to visit me could stay there. Just down the street. On the corner. In a neat little older brick house I'd fixed up. A little privacy for the guest; a little privacy for me.

Of course. In seven years I'd had only one visitor from outside of Box Elder County. A guy I knew from high school. Not even a good friend really. A couple of years older than me. Driving through. Out on the freeway. Heard that I lived in the area. Called me up. I invited him to stop. We had a couple of beers. It got late. He was in no particular hurry so I told him to stay. I put him on a futon in my home office. I made sandwiches for dinner. When I told him that I owned the house outright had no mortgage—he was disturbed. I mean. I really had no interest in discussing it with him. But he was asking. Interested in housing in the area and what it cost.

—You paid cash?

—Yeah.

—That's crazy. Don't you realize how much money you're throwing away?

—You mean.

—With mortgages at what? Four percent? You can make three times that on the stock market. Look. Let me put you in touch with a guy. My financial manager. He can help you with this.

—Yeah.

—My wife and I. He showed us what to do. When we had extra money he invested it for us. Told us not to pay off our house. He helped us refinance. Got a great interest rate. Put the rest in the market. You know seven percent minimum. We're figuring to double our money.

—Great.

—You'd be stupid not to. Look. This guy is a Christian. Great guy. I'll give him your name. He'll really put your money to work.

—Uh-huh.

—He's been talking to us lately about real estate. Take some of our cash and leverage it. Get a good mortgage. Buy a house. Rent it. The rent pays the mortgage. When the market goes up you sell. Make a killing. You're out basically nothing. If you've got some money to get started you're in the driver's seat.

—Wow.

He went on like that until bed time. I yawned widely three or four times. Finally I got up and wished him good night. In the morning I very heartily wished him the best. A lot of wishing. I pushed him out the door. I told him to come again. But. Of course. I hoped I would never see him again. What a dope.

20

It seems that most houses today are constructed with trussed roof frames constructed off-site. The trusses are delivered to the building site on a flatbed. They are installed with a lift or crane. It isn't a bad system really. You can see how it is more efficient than cutting every joist and jack from scratch.

For the house breaker though I'm not sure. I mean. I've never tried to take a custom-cut roof apart rafter by rafter. But the trusses are kind of tricky when you're working by yourself and without a crane. The system I developed—if you can call it that—relied mostly on gravity. With the exception of the first couple trusses on the end I attempted to control the crash. But. As a matter of fact many of the trusses twisted and broke on impact. It was not my intention to be destructive but it was simply the shortest route to removing the house.

I'd spend an entire Saturday over there. Keeping the remainder of the trusses tied together for stability I'd break the first one—the one on the end the gable truss—free from the wall. With nothing below it I'd let it topple over. Generally that first one would break apart on the ground. I'd go down and disassemble it. That took a while. With a saw and a crowbar I'd sort it into several piles. Those with metal and those without. I'd pull nails and screws. Toss them in a bucket. Anytime I could get a clean piece of wood of at least eight feet in length I'd set it aside in a pile. This was good salvage.

For the truss plates—the gussets—the only thing I could think of was to put them in the campfire. I'd make a little pit in the yard and start a fire. It would burn the lumber off the plates. Then I'd let the fire go out. In a day or two I'd go and fish the blackened plates out of the pit. It was a dirty way to do it. But I'd throw the plates in a bucket. It would all go to Roberts at $50 a ton.

On a Saturday in July I was plugging away at the task. Another vehicle pulled up. I looked over. It was Michelle's hatchback. She knew—of course—about the project. We'd talked about it. Looked at it a couple of times. But she'd never come on a work day. I wasn't sure what to think. She got out and stood looking at me over the door of her car. She was a sight for sore eyes.

—What's going on?

—I thought I'd stop by. Check on your progress.

—Not much progress.

—Can I help?

—I don't know.

I put down my tools and went over to her. I took one hip in each hand and leaned my cheek against hers. I was dirty. A little sweaty. I wasn't sure what to do with her. I was used to working by myself. I preferred it. I didn't mind the solitude at all. It gave me time to think.

—Hey.

—Hey.

—Do you want to stack that lumber for me?

—Yeah. I can do that.

—Have you got gloves?

—I don't.

—Here. I've got an extra pair. All these pieces. I'm going to keep them. At least for now. I'm putting them in a stack. Over here. They're not too heavy. You can just grab one. And stack it. Like this.

I showed her. She did the next one.

—Quick learner.

She gave me an annoyed look. Then she went and got another board.

I went back to what I'd been doing. I'd got about half-way down a truss—pulling nails and cutting away the plates—when I could feel her looking at me. I stopped and looked over. All the loose lumber was stacked.

—What now?

—OK. See all those broken and cut pieces with plates on them?

—Yeah.

—You can pick them up and put them in that pile of ashes over there.

She made short work of that too.

—OK. How about coming over here and helping me get another one of these down?

For the trusses in the middle of the building I had set up a rope that allowed me to lower them—lean them topple them—until they were either lying flat on top of the walls or completely inverted inside of them. From there I could slide them down the walls to the end and let them drop to the ground or slide them to the floor and drag them out between the wall studs.

—Here. Stand here. Hold this. When I get it loose you're going to let out the rope until the top of the truss has flipped 180 degrees and is pointed at the floor.

I got up on the wall and pried on the bracing. Piece by piece I worked the truss free. It started to wobble.

—OK. Here it comes.

Michelle started lowering. Too fast. Instead of a cautious hand over hand she was letting the rope zip through her gloves. The truss rolled over completely. With some velocity. This caused it to go past the vertical and to swing up towards her. She dropped the rope completely and jumped back. One of the truss chords—now upside down—slipped off the wall. The peak of the truss hit the floor and the whole thing pivoted pulling the other side off the wall. It stopped—a little twisted—with one chord pointing out the end and the other pointing at her. It happened fast. A second or two at most. I could only watch from on top of the wall.

—Oh. I'm so sorry. I'm sorry.

—I just don't want you to get hit.

—I guess I didn't understand what I was doing. I'm sorry.

—It's OK. It happens to me all the time. I'm taking it apart. Remember? I don't care what happens to it. I just don't want anyone to get hit.

I climbed down and went over to her. I put my arms around her from the back. I leaned my face against the side of her neck.

—Let's go over to the house and get something to eat. I'm hungry.

—I'm really sorry.

—Stop saying that.

When you file for bankruptcy the court appoints a trustee. The trustee disposes of assets and satisfies creditors under the direction of the court. Well. Most creditors probably wind up dissatisfied. They are undoubtedly required to accept a haircut. Pennies back on the dollar.

Douglas West. Mr. West. Douglas West, Esq. This was the trustee. I looked it up on the internet. He was an attorney. Of course. I called his office.

—Hello. My name is John Smith. I'm calling for Mr. West.

—Speaking.

I was surprised. I thought he'd be a big shot partner or something. I was planning to work my way up the phone tree. Through the phalanx of gate keepers. I was caught a little off guard.

—Um. I'm calling to make an offer on some bankrupt property. I mean. The property is owned by some folks who filed for bankruptcy. The court documents show that you are the trustee.

—Yeah. What's the name?

—Ewell. Rick and Amy. Ewell. Or maybe Johnston?

—Hang on. Let me look it up.

I hung on. I could hear fingers on the keyboard.

—OK. Yeah. I've got it here. Rick and Amy. That's right. What is the property.

—Well. They've been living at this place. I'm assuming they own it. I'd like to buy it.

—The house?

—Yeah.

—Let's see. Yeah. They've declared the house. It appears to be one of their assets.

—May I make an offer on it?

—You may.

—Can I email it? Or snail mail? Is there a way that you'd prefer?

—No. Either is fine.

—And you have the authority to sign the offer?

He laughed.

—This isn't going to happen fast. Yeah. I can sign the offer. But it has to be approved by the court. And—to some extent—by the creditors. I'll have to get some title work done too.

—So the creditors have to approve the sale?

—No. But they have an interest in maximizing the value of any asset that I sell. Let's just say that I'm sensitive to that.

—Got it. May I ask you one more question?

—Of course.

—There is no mortgage on the house. How can you be bankrupt when you own your house? Outright. They moved out. Moved somewhere. Why? I thought there had been a foreclosure.

West laughed again.

—Good question. I've wondered that myself. They have a number of problems. Including with the IRS. And the total debt they have accumulated is not small. They may have felt that they couldn't save the house. They may have received numerous phone calls. In fact I'm sure they did. Some of them may have seemed quite threatening.

—So where did they go?

—I believe they are living with one of his relatives.

My girlfriend. That is what she was. She was my girlfriend. Michelle was. It seemed strange to me. To call her that. To use the word. But it was undeniable. The amount of time we spent together. The conversations we had. The things we did. It had become obvious to our colleagues. People around the office knew that we were dating. It was OK. I guess. I mean. You're not supposed to have relationships at work. Right? What is going to happen when you break up? But. It was OK. It really was. I'd have to wait to cross any unpleasant future bridges. But for now. For now. It was kind of nice. She was actually a good girlfriend. So far. She seemed to take me for what I was. And I was sometimes unpleasant—I could have a short temper and a sharp tongue. I kept expecting her to tell me something unacceptable about me. Maybe describe her perfect partner. In a way that made it clear that I was lacking something. Perhaps many things. But she never did.

She was also patient and optimistic. Patient meaning that she could put up with things. Not fly off the handle. Not over-react. She could handle a setback or a frustration without a lot of drama. No drama with her. No temper tantrums. Optimistic meaning that her first assumption was always that things were OK. Things were good. She never assumed the worst. Her outlook was generally sunny. Cheerful. That is the word. She was cheerful most of the time. She got out of bed in the morning with a smile.

Her personality was a benefit to me: I can be angry; I can be sharp tongued; I can be a bit of a jerk; I can be critical; I can be impatient with foolishness. I admit to over-reacting at times. I'm pessimistic about certain things. If Michelle had been the kind of person to over-react to my over-reactions it wouldn't have worked out. I don't mean to say that she was some kind of Pollyanna—turning every hard topic or hard experience into a joke or a game. That wouldn't have worked out either. But her default approach to things was one of patient good cheer.

A person who is patient and optimistic and cheerful isn't likely to be a grudge holder. Michelle wasn't. A grudge holder. Which was fortunate. Because we got into arguments sometimes. We had a few fights. We went home early and angry sometimes. Mostly it was my fault. I'd say something caustic. Something highly critical. About her. About someone else. She felt it was unfair. And it probably was. Or her feelings were hurt. So she said something back. Something angry. Something intended to be a bit of a jab. And I took her up on it. And we went back and forth. Said some things. Mostly true things. But angry things. Intended for winning. Winning the argument. One-upping.

The first time it happened I was pretty irritated. I went home and thought about it for a long time. About how she shouldn't have said some things; about how I shouldn't have said some things. I was pretty put-out. But then I repented of my irritation and went to bed. In the morning I was worried. I didn't want to be angry with her. I didn't want to be fighting with her. But how were we going to get past it? I could apologize. Sure. But what if she wouldn't accept an apology? Couldn't let it go?

I needn't have worried. She stopped by my office at coffee time. It had become a bit of a pattern. Coffee time that is. She looked straight at me.

Her face was normal. Cheerful.

She spoke first.

—Hey.

—Hey.

—I'm sorry for getting angry and saying that stuff last night.

I laughed. With relief. With great relief. I was thrilled. With relief.

—I accept your apology. But it was mostly my fault. I started it. And I was a jerk about it. And some of what I said was pretty bad too. I was wrong to do it. I hope you'll accept my apology?

The last part was stilted. It caught a little in my throat. But I wanted to put it out there. There is nothing worse than someone who can't admit when they are in the wrong.

—Of course I will. You were kind of a jerk. But I like you too much to spend a lot of time fighting with you.

—I like you too.

Right then I wanted to get up and show her how much. But we were at work. So I simply offered to help with the coffee break.

—Let me buy the hot chocolate this morning.

21

Let me live where I will, on this side is the city, on that the wilderness, and ever I am leaving the city more and more and withdrawing to the wilderness.

Henry Thoreau

This is the other thing about them. The developers. Or the buyers. I don't know which of them is to blame. Do the developers do it because the buyers want it or do the buyers buy it because the developers do it? Anyway. Have you ever noticed how the whole thing is about fake interior luxury? I mean marble countertops from Italy. Or somewhere. Those would be great. Yeah. But even if we can't we can have it we can have something that looks like it. That is important. Wood floors. Or I don't know. Imported tile floors. Those would be good. Yeah. But even if we can't we can have it we can have something that looks like it. En suite. What is it? I don't know. I don't know what it means. But even if we can't have it we can have something that looks like it. All our money spent on it. A quarter of a million. A half a million. That is what we spend. Or what we want to spend. And even if we can't have it we can have something that looks like it.

But here is the thing. All of the fake luxury is interior. Interior. The exterior has some fake flourishes too. It is true. But the exterior is just an accident. The last two days of the two months put into flinging the house onto the dirt. Roll down a square of turf. Put some gravel in the ditch from the street. A plastic window box. Something.

But this is all secondary. Tertiary. When we've run out of fake-lux creativity inside we turn to the outside. And then we throw up some

129

plastic. Run some PVC. Some gravel. A retaining wall. Something. Something stupid and ill conceived.

So you look on Zillow. On Realtor dot com. The place goes for $400,000. There are 26 pictures. All of them of the interior. Look at these under-counter LCD lights! The master en suite tile iphone charger with dual granite satellite dishes from Italy! OMG. I think I just soiled myself. But when you got to the end of the 26 pictures you've never seen outdoors. You don't know if the place is at Canary Warf or Aspen Mountain.

When you drive over there you will find one of two things. It will either be a development with tenth acre lots. In which case your half million dollar dream home will fill the entire lot. Except for the square strip of turf in front. Or. It will be a suburb with three acre lots. In which case the dream home will squat in a sea of sage brush. Except for the square strip of turf in front and the debris that the concrete guy dumped between the road and the front walkway that points from the door to nowhere.

What does this say? It says—for one thing—that Americans are completely divorced from the natural world. Nothing about our lives would ever require us to go outdoors. But it also says that Americans don't build to fit our surroundings. Our surroundings are irrelevant. We don't even notice them. Who cares? We never go out anyway. Unless we're driving.

Sometimes I look at them. I do. I think about buying them. Not to break but to live in. I do. I think about it because I am looking for something new. A change. I see a place on ten acres out in the valley. It looks kind of nice. I can probably work out how to afford it. I think about it. I look at it on Realtor. Finally I drive out there. In under 30 seconds I've rejected it. Turned around. Forgotten about it. Moved on. Why? Because it doesn't fit the landscape. It is an eye-sore. The roof is red. The walls are blue plastic. The lawn is green and square.

Can no one see this? Why not a little low cabin of native stone? Maybe some of the local shrubs preserved during construction. Something easy on the eyes. Something that doesn't interrupt the sweep of light across the valley.

Ah. No. I'm a fool. Why have that when we can have fake interior luxury?

Late in the summer when the weather was clear and cool I took Michelle to a place. It was twenty or thirty miles off the pavement. Then. Another four or five miles up a wash. Hardly a road at all. Then. On foot. Up a little draw. Narrow. A few small dry falls. Around some boulders. Into a little cove. A sandy floor with a couple of large pines. In the wash there were a few small pools left over from the last storm. We carried our sleeping bags. I went back to the truck for another load—food wine the stove. In the afternoon we sat together reading in the shade. Saying nothing. At dusk we opened the wine. At dark I made a small fire in the sand out of bark twigs duff fallen from the pines. We ate a couple of sandwiches and sat in front of it. Michelle sat on my lap.

In the morning I got up quietly. Michelle was still asleep. Her head inside the sleeping bag. I climbed out of the cove—up a ramp of sandstone. At the top I walked across a flat covered with pinyon. I reached another draw with ledges on both sides. I went up the draw until I could climb one of the ledges. I was on a fairly large plateau. Made of rock. Where the rock had cracked pinyon sprouted. And juniper. And bitterbrush. I walked around the cracks and crossed the plateau. I was facing east. It was chilly. But the light was growing. I waited. I looked across the country to another plateau. Higher. With Douglas fir and ponderosa pine in the little coves along the rim. I heard the call of the wren. It was still. Then the first ray of sun hit me. I put on my sunglasses. Within minutes the world turned from monochrome to blazing color— from dusk to day. A slight breeze moved up the hill and across the plateau. It felt cold. I felt cold. But only briefly. Within minutes the heat from the sun was working into my clothes. My sweatshirt and hat were warm to the touch. The chill was gone from my face and hands.

I went back to the camp. Michelle was still hidden in the bag. I carefully started the stove. Put the pot on for coffee water. She turned and pull the cloth away from her face. Her eyes her mouth were fresh from sleep. She smiled.

—How'd you do last night?

—Great. You?

—OK. Were you warm enough?

—I was. How long have you been up?

—Not long. Forty-five minutes.

I put the coffee in the press and got out the cups. When the water was hot I poured it and let it steep. I went over and laid down on top of her. On top of the sleeping bag. She turned—arms out—and hugged me. I kissed her on the mouth.

—Ready for coffee?

—Yeah. Thanks for brewing.

I poured two cups and brought one to her. She sat up with her legs in the bag. She put on a coat and hat. The sun had not yet penetrated our shaded cove. I sat back and looked at her.

—What do you want to do today?

—I don't know. Hike. Explore. I've never seen this place. You?

—Yeah. When we're ready we can go back down to the main wash— where we left the truck—and hike upstream.

I got up and took the water off the stove. I replaced the pot with a small pan. I got a couple of home-made—but frozen—breakfast burritos from the little cooler I'd carried up the day before. I covered them with a piece of foil and put them in the pan. I refilled the coffee cups.

—You grew up doing this?

—Yeah. Well. Not like this. My Dad liked to take us out camping. But he had a subdue-the-wilderness mentality. He carried old world war style trenching tools. Saws. Hatchets. Setting up camp required a lot of digging cutting hacking pounding nailing trenching building. You'd have a wilderness style kitchen table. A clothes line. A potty. A big tent.

Michelle laughed.

—Yeah. But it was still fun wasn't it?

—It was. Dad taught me a lot about enjoying the outdoors.

—You're lucky. My parents. Never.

—Not outdoor people huh?

—My Mom has never slept outdoors in her life. My Dad maybe. But we were a suburban family. Plain and simple. Indoor people. I didn't sleep out until I was a college camp counselor. And even then it was inside a screened cabin.

After a while we went down the draw. Back to where we'd left the truck. The sun was higher now but it was still pleasant in the shade. Not hot. We stopped at the truck and refilled our water bottles. We walked up the wash. We came—right away—to a small ledge. Vertical. Six or eight feet high. Not difficult to surmount by climbing up the side but difficult for an ATV or a jeep—impossible in fact. There was trash. There always is. But without motorized access there was less. I'm not saying foot traffic isn't trashy traffic. It often is. I've stepped over dirty diapers discarded on hiking trails. But without a motor to make it easy you don't transport a lot of trash very far.

We walked for three or four hours. Not fast. Just picking our way. Around and over large blocks fallen from the wall. Through brushy stands of willow and salt cedar on damp sandbars. Every curve in the creek was a new exploration. Sometimes there were blind arches. Sometimes tiny trickling waterfalls—the stream soon disappearing into the cobble. Except for the hourly jet traffic in and out of Las Vegas—which I did my best to ignore—it was quiet. There were a couple of tricky dry-falls—conquered by going back and finding a broken slope that let us out above the obstacle. By early afternoon we were five or six miles above the truck and beneath a towering fall—80 or 100 feet at least. It was sandy and there was a pool. We called it a day. We stopped there in the shade at the edge of the pool and ate a sandwich. We drank the rest of our water. We rested.

The afternoon sun was hot. We walked slowly. Steadily. Not speaking. Retracing our tracks from the morning We saw no one. Heard nothing. It was still. We reached the truck in the late afternoon. Sat in its shade drinking water. I collected some food and another bottle of wine from the cooler. We climbed back to our camp.

We went to bed early that night. Michelle was tired from the hike; sleepy from the wine. I wasn't. I lay in my sleeping bag looking up through the branches of a pine. The sky was dark violet—aged on the lees of the setting sun. A planet—Venus? Mars?—was visible from where I lay. The Vegas airport traffic was absent for now. The evening breeze had died to stillness. A few stars began to appear. As I lay there I began to hear something—something extremely rare: It was silence. It surprised me a little—finding it there. I held my breath. Silence. Perfect silence. Roaring deafening silence. Oh! Joy!

Actually the house on the corner was not for sale. And I didn't really have the money to buy it. It was more of a project for the future. I didn't even know the owner. Whoever owned it didn't live there. Lived in California or something. It was a rental.

When I first moved into the neighborhood the tenant was an older lady. Quiet. Clean. Peaceful. The yard was picked up. She went in and out every few days or so. Drove up and down the street. To the grocery. 20 MPH. Friendly wave.

I never spoke with her. I assumed she owned the place. I assumed we were friends. In the way that neighbors are friends. Never speaking. Always waving. But sensing that we know something about each other. Knowing where we live. Knowing where we belong. And being content with it. Content that your neighbors don't live like pigs—that they pay their bills and pick up their shit.

Then. One weekend there were a bunch of pickup trucks over there. Four or five guys. Younger guys. Sons? Grandsons? Nephews? Back and forth from the house to the yard. Out came the sofa. A couple of mattresses. Boxes. They worked at it all weekend. On Monday the place was empty. Windows bare. No lights in the evening. No car in the drive. She'd moved out.

A FOR RENT sign went in the front window. I didn't see who put it there. But it turned out to be the end of the peace and quiet. I may have mentioned that the place was a little ramshackle. Well. The rent must have been low. Because low renters became common. Not staying long. Three months. Six. Sometimes just weeks.

I don't know. I don't know why you'd want to run a rental like that. I can assume that it is probably all about getting that monthly rent check. Who cares what the tenant looks like—whether they wipe their asses. But the constant turnover must be hard on your financial planning. I don't know. Maybe they pay first and last month's rent. Stay a few weeks. And you keep it all. Maybe it's a good business.

In any case it is bad for the neighborhood. Bad for my neighborhood. Probably most people don't care. But I do. There are some things I don't like. Noise and trash are two of them. When you've got a low rent rental you're going to have both.

And I don't have anything against people who can't afford a lot of rent. We've all been there. Been out of work. Been a student. Been a Mexican. Working for a pretty small wage. Cleaning. Serving. Sweeping up at the construction site. I know how it is. I have a lot of respect for that. Sometimes people are having a tough time making ends meet. Maybe there is a family. Kids. Gotta pay for transportation to get to work. Gas prices are high. Gotta put food on the table. I know. You can't pay a lot of rent. I've been between jobs. I've lived in closets. I've slept on couches. I've ordered coffee and a donut and—like Joe Christmas—had to give the coffee back.

But that isn't what I'm talking about. This place wasn't attracting the low rent workers. The ones trying to make ends meet. Busy. Working. Trying to take responsibility for themselves. No. This place was attracting the deadbeats. The slobs. The thugs. The petty criminals. No job and no evident effort to find one.

They came and went. Fortunately. Some of them were better than others. The single moms usually weren't too bad. Unless they had a lot of boyfriends. I mean. I don't know what is going on when there is a different car parked over there every day. And the kids. Three. Four. Five-years-old. On the street. Walking up and down. Screeching. Fighting. No place to go. No one looking after them. I can see a Jeep pulled up in front of the place. By the time I finish mowing the lawn the Jeep is gone. The next day it's a souped-up Accord. You know. I think there was a movie about those. Vin Diesel. Little race cars for the urban thug wanna-be. The babies are on the street again. The next day it's a mini-van. Hey. I don't know. I don't really care. Although it does annoy me that the visitors drive 80 MPH in the street. Sometimes you can hear them coming. They turn off the highway three blocks away. They floor it. You can hear the fast and furious shifting. They go by so fast it lifts your gas clippings off the street. Their feet are already on the brake. Hard. They park. Slouch to the door. Here come the little kids. Playing in the street for a couple hours. Don't ask me what is going on. I don't want to know.

By far the worst though were the semi-family units with a loser male or two attached to the household in some capacity. Generally there would be females and kids too. But I don't know that they were ever the ring leaders. These guys would be working on their cars in the yard. Pretty soon there would be three or four of them. Or more. None of them visibly employed. But all of them able to afford cigarettes. And beer. And gas for their cars.

Some of the cars nicer than what I could buy. Driving back and forth. Forty times a day. Or sometimes walking. I don't know why. Pants down the ass. Hats backward. Cigarettes hanging from the mouth. Just slouching along. Got all day. Got it made.

Usually that species of renter would turn up with dogs. Pit bulls. Or something exotic and aggressive. Barking a lot. Up and down the street with the dogs. I remember working in the garden one day. I saw one of those guys go by with the dog. On a bicycle. The thug was on the bike; the dog was on the leash. The dog—untrained and undisciplined—lunged at something and pulled the thug off the bike. He went down on the asphalt. Hard. He was up in an instant. Bounced. Practically. He beat the crap out of the dog. Cursing it viciously. Punching and kicking. Whipping it with the leash. Then he got back on the bicycle. The dog—confused and cowering—jerked away from him. He went down again. Got up. Beat the shit out of the dog. Got back on the bike. They went down the street like that.

Eventually one of those groups revealed to me the source of their beer money. At least some of it. I'd been at work. In fact I'd been at work a lot. And out with Michelle. I'd been busy. Not at home much. But finally I got around to mowing my yard. I went to the shed for the mower. The mower wasn't there. I looked all over the place for it. I walked over to the old Roundy property to see if I'd left it there. I was confused. Then I noticed that my rototiller was gone too. And an old mountain bike I had.

For the next couple of days I drove around my neighborhood with my eyes open. Eventually I realized that there were two or three odd rototillers in the back yard of the rental—with the pit bulls. I went to the City Chief of Police. Kevin. Kevin Adams. In his flak jacket. He knew right away what I was talking about.

—Oh. Yeah. Those punks. But I'll need to get a search warrant.

I told him the make and model of my tiller. I even managed to find a warrantee document on it from the time I bought it. Two days later Kevin called me at work.

—I've got your tiller.

—Thanks. Was it at that place?

—Yeah.

—Any lawn mowers? Bikes?

—No. They must have moved those already.

—Were they there?

—No. There was a young lady there. She said that her ex-boyfriend used to hang around with some dirt-bags. But she said that she'd broken up with him and kicked them all out.

—Uh-huh.

—I've run into her before. And I know who this boyfriend is. There is an outstanding warrant for him from the state drug task force. With your report and the information I got from the girl I've doubled it. Everybody in the state will be looking for him now. It is a sizeable warrant.

—What about the other guys?

—Oh. Them. Yeah. We know most of them. Young. Stupid. In with the wrong crowd. Petty stuff. Petty. I mean. I know it doesn't make you feel any better. But these are just low level losers. Drop outs. Semi-homeless. Kicked out by their parents. You know.

—Then how do they afford the cars the gas the dogs the beer?

—I don't know. Selling some drugs. Stealing and selling stuff from around the neighborhood. Nothing violent or anything. But we know who they are. And now they know we're looking for them. They'll probably lay low for a while. You won't have to worry about them anymore. When they surface again we'll pick them up.

He sounded a little bit over confident to me. They'd been kicked out huh? By the "ex" girlfriend. Ex my ass. It seemed like a good thing for the young lady to tell the cop when he banged on her door in the morning. By the evening the thugs would be back in the yard.

Sure enough. I was right. There they were that afternoon. When I got home from work I could hear the thump thump of the hip hop music. I could see them coming and going. They started a bonfire and were out there half the night. So much for the warrant. So much for every cop in the state looking to pick them up.

But I was also wrong. Within two weeks the place was vacant again. I never did see what happened. Maybe they just found a better place. I don't know. Maybe Kevin arrested the ring leader. Maybe the ex-girlfriend really did send them packing. I don't know. It was fine with me though. The FOR RENT sign went back in the window.

That is when I started thinking about buying the place. Buying it for my business. Not because I really wanted it. But because I wanted to close the halfway house for deadbeats.

22

It ain't anybody perfect on this green earth of God's, preachers nor nobody else.

Flannery O'Connor

My uncle was on his way through town. Passing by on his way to Texas. Where he lived. Now. Used to have a hay farm out here. A cabin on the mountain. I don't know. Don't understand it. If you've got a couple hundred acres of hay and a cabin on the mountain why do you move to Texas? Retire. He retired to Texas. If I had some hay ground and a cabin on the mountain I'd never retire. Especially to Texas. Arlington Texas.

He and my aunt stopped on their way through. Wanted to buy me lunch. Taking the freeway. Down to Albuquerque I guess. El Paso. Odessa. Abilene. Fort Worth. Like a Little Feat song or something. Tucumcari? No. Not on that route.

Lunch turned into two hours. Two hours of talking. Not me. I didn't say anything. But I learned a lot about my uncle. I learned that he never really was a farmer. All those years. He was just a tourist in disguise. I was surprised. Dismayed. A consumer. A consumer of semi-luxo-drive-by-freeway-exit-attractions. He'd rather be on a cruise than on the farm. Rather be at the buffet than eating a sandwich on the tailgate of the truck. Rather be at the track putting five on the grey to place than on the porch at the cabin listening to the wrens. He turned out to be a real American. His mind seemingly empty. It hurt me. It really did. But there was no sense saying anything. No sense bringing up something I'd seen—even if I could get a word in edgewise—because the only things I ever see are coyotes skittering off the road into the oak brush and the chaff coming off a baler when I take the back-road home from work.

—Now over to Fort Worth you've got more of the cowboy scene. You know. Horns on the Cadillac. Saloons. Rodeos. I can see how a cowboy would get a whole lot of enjoyment out of Fort Worth.

—Uh-huh.

—The world's largest saloon is there. Over to Fort Worth. It is really something. A stage in the middle of it all. They bring in the biggest acts. You can see. I don't know. All the big country music stars there.

—Great.

—And the ribs. And the baked potatoes. With everything. I eat that whole potato and can't finish my ribs. Have to bring 'em home.

—Yeah.

—We go out to eat a lot now. There are a lot of good restaurants. When we were getting ready to retire I was reluctant to move. But I wouldn't want to be anywhere else. Texas has everything.

—Yeah.

—Sometimes we go over to the track. Horse track. There is a race every twenty minutes. Horse races. Can you believe that? I like to put a little money on the horses. I don't know. I guess some people call it gambling. She doesn't like us going there.

He nodded at his wife. My aunt.

—She thinks we're going to run into somebody from our church. Our church is right near there. She gets nervous. Thinks somebody will see us. Heck. I don't care. They've got free entrance and free Pepsi for seniors on Saturdays. I like going there every week. Besides. Like I always tell her. If somebody from church is going to see us it will be because they're in there too. If they don't say anything to the pastor we won't either.

He laughed. I laughed too.

—Did you know that Arlington—where we live—is home to the Cowboys? The Mavericks? It's great. We live right next to Cowboys Stadium. AT&T Stadium.

—Wow.

I couldn't think of anything else to say. I couldn't think of anything worse than living next to Cowboys Stadium. I would slit my wrists. I would chew glass. It made me depressed just thinking about it. As I thought about it I felt a little like Mary-Grace—maybe they'd put me in the sylum.

—Right next door to that. Sharing the parking lot even. Is seven flags. Or is it six?

He turned to look at his wife. My aunt. But didn't stop talking.

—Anyway. I can't remember how many flags. Big amusement park. You know. Great for the kids. Water slides and all that.

For some reason that prelude from the Proverbs of Solomon popped into my head. *These six things doth the Lord hate: yea, seven are an abomination unto him.*

—Besides that. We've got lakes. We live just half a mile from Arlington Lake. Actually closer than that. But you've got to go to the end of the block and take a left to get to the boat ramp. Now I've just got buy a boat.

He looked at my aunt.

—Bass boat. That is the kind of place for a bass boat. Probably can get one for six or seven thousand. Used. You know. I'd really like a pontoon boat. But we don't have the space to park it.

He glanced her way.

—We've got to buy her some furniture too.

He looked over at me again.

—We've been sitting on some hand-me-down sofas in the living room. But she wants some new furniture. What time is it anyway?

I looked at my watch.

—Well it was great to visit with you.

—Yeah.

When they were gone. I went back to work. Back to my office. I closed the door and put my head down on a corner of the desk. I was so depressed. My heart felt empty. Goddamned bass boat. Cowboys Stadium. I almost started crying.

After submitting my offer on the Ewell house I heard nothing for a couple of weeks. Then West called with a problem.

—The wife—Amy—was married to a guy named Johnston.

—Yeah. I heard about that. I guess he was killed in an accident.

—Oh. I didn't know how he died. Well. The Johnston's made a number of conveyances back and forth. They did this with quit claim deeds. I'm not sure what the point was. Amy's mother was involved in some of it. It may have been a way to offload some debt. Or to pay back loans within the family. Anyway they did it two or three times. But they didn't use an attorney.

—Uh-huh.

—As a result none of the deeds uses the term "joint tenant." Nor are the conveyances described as between "husband and wife." Which makes it appear that the property may have been held in common.

—OK.

—Sorry to bore you with all this. But if they were joint tenants—which married people generally are—the entire property would pass to her—to Amy—at his death. If not his portion of the property would be retained as part of his estate.

—Yeah.

—Because there is no proof that they were joint tenants his interest in the property may not have passed to her at the time of his death.

—Which means that she may not own the whole property.

—That's right. His portion of the property may belong to his heirs whoever they may be. I don't know. She may be his only heir. But I don't know yet.

—So you're telling me that I am trying to buy a house owned by a dead guy?

West laughed.

—Something like that. The thing is. What they needed to do at the time of his death was to have his estate probated. Do you know if they did that?

—I don't know. But based on what you've told me about the deeds. And based on what I've seen of her attitude. I'm not sure they were the most professional and proactive people in the world.

—You're right. Which means that there probably was no probate at the time of his death and we currently don't know who owns his interest in the house.

—So what can we do?

—Well. Lawyers are specialists. And so are judges. Which means that we—the judge and I—know what to do about bankruptcy but we are not experts on probate. We need to obtain an opinion on whether the current Ms. Ewell is the sole owner of the house or whether Mr. Johnston retains an interest. The court has authorized a modest expenditure and I've used it to hire a probate specialist.

—Oh boy.

—Yeah. So we need to give him a couple of weeks or a month to work. He'll need to review the whole case and submit a written opinion to the court.

—If he finds that the house is Ewell's will you be able to sell it to me?

—I don't know. The judge has not ruled on that part of the process. I'm assuming that we can proceed but I can't say for certain until we get this cleared up.

—What does the Lutheran church say about pre-marital sex?

We were at my house. In my bed. It was early in the evening. Maybe seven. We'd been making dinner together. We'd tried to eat some of the dinner. But we were impatient. So dinner was interrupted for thirty minutes in the bed.

—Is that what we just had?

—Yeah. I think so.

—Pre-marital?

—Oh. I don't know. I guess so. Extra-marital then.

—They're against it.

—So what about you?

She laughed.

—I'm against it too.

—The only thing you're against right now is me.

She laughed again. Pushing me away.

—I don't know. I shouldn't be here probably.

—But you are.

—I know. I'm insecure.

—What do you mean?

—I love you. I want to be with you. This is part of it.

—You think I'd kick you out if you didn't?

—I don't know.

—I wouldn't.

—What about that place you go to?

—What place? I kind of bounce around.

—Do any of them approve of extra-marital sex?

—No. It might lead to dancing. Or card playing.

Another laugh. An old joke.

—So. Why are you?

—Well. First of all. I'm not a church member. I'm still trying to find a place where I fit.

—But nowhere you go is going to want you doing this.

—I know. But after years of trying to follow all the little personal pieties of American fundamentalist evangelicalism I've mostly given up.

—You're not a Christian?

—Oh I don't know. All I know is that Jesus said that harlots would enter the kingdom of heaven before Pharisees. I've started to think that there are worse things than plain old human sin. Self-righteousness for example.

—You're starting to sound like Walker Percy.

—If only. I mean. I've had people tell me that they are trying to get the victory over cursing. Oh. Shit. I always say. I'll let you know when I get to that. Right now I'm trying to keep from being angry envious greedy murderous and vindictive.

—Come on?

—No really. I can admit that I'm a self-centered jerk. Cursing is the least of my worries.

—So?

—So. This is probably wrong. But I'm going to be saved by grace alone or I'm going to go to hell.

—Now you're sounding like a Lutheran.

—Grace alone?

—Yeah.

When I was a kid—back in New England—houses had foundations. With basements. Cellars. Newer foundations were made of concrete. But the old ones were stone. Rock. Stacked stone or rock foundations. With dirt floor cellars. The house where I lived as a kid had one. A stone foundation. With a cellar. Dirt floor.

I'm not saying it was good. I don't know. It was moldy. Sometimes it flooded. It was mildewy. My Dad stored some tools in the cellar. They rusted. But it was kind of fun. As a kid. Down in the cellar playing in the cool and damp. There was a massive old oil burning furnace down there. Bunker fuel. It burned bunker fuel. I don't know. Maybe not. But it was old. The stuff they pumped into it looked like liquid asphalt. The furnace whooshed and rattled and blew. It smelled like west Texas. In the summer that huge old furnace turned into an air conditioner. Well. Not the furnace but the blower. Dad would go down and remove the filter. Open the furnace door. Then he would turn on the blower. Whoosh. The cold wet air from the cellar would pump through the duct work and fill the house.

Anyway. They don't make 'em like that anymore. At least not in the west. Not in the new developments. Not the plastic houses that are installed in weeks. A couple of months at most. For that there are slabs. Houses are built on slabs. Slabs of concrete. The Ewell house. Built on a slab. The more of the house I removed; the more of the slab I exposed. Some cracks in it. Running like webs across the floor. But not bad. Still flat. Not as bad as some others I've seen. Settling and cracking. Buckling. The corner raising like the prow of a ship. Things you drop skittering downhill.

On Tuesday I left for the offices of our parent company. In San Diego. All of our designers were centralized there. When it was time to design and format a book everything went to San Diego. I was ready for cover art on the Rauschenbusch biography so I took it there. San Diego is a little too far to drive for a one day meeting. So I flew. I started at the county airport. Which I don't mind. The parking is free. The terminal is tiny. There is just one flight per day. The TSA screeners know everyone. Low stress. Easy. Show up 10 minutes before the flight.

I flew to the hub. Las Vegas. It took about an hour. Have I mentioned that I hate Las Vegas? Anyway. I walked up one concourse and down the next. I found my second flight. When it came time to board I took my seat on the aisle and tried to read. It was difficult. The rest of the world was trying to board in a timely manner. But there is no longer space on a commercial aircraft for the average American and his two "carry-on" bags.

First there is the average American or I should say there is the mammoth American. You know he isn't going to fit in his seat and he is going to take half of yours. And I shouldn't limit this to men or even adults. Second there is the "carry-on." Why bother calling it that? These things cannot be carried. They are the size of a farm wagon. The first one takes up the overhead bin for the entire row and requires its owner to solicit the help of two of the three stewardesses to lift it that high. What is in those things anyway? I mean the American uniform is shorts flip-flops and tattoos. What can be in the luggage? More flip-flops? More tattoos?

To be fair the airlines have caused this by a) charging very high fees to check your luggage and b) failing to enforce the "carry-on" size rule. People have learned that you won't have to pay the hundred dollar luggage fee if you just roll right up to the door of the airplane with your piano dolly. They'll either let you stuff it in the overhead bin or they will pink tag it for a free gate-check.

I had reserved a rental car in San Diego. So I went to the Enterprise desk and gave them my ID. The guy apologized for not having the economy car I'd reserved and asked if I could accept a free upgrade. While I waited I watched the TV. Fucking TV. If you're travelling in modern America the television is going to be everywhere. It is in the car the plane the airport the hotel the restaurant the kitchen the bedroom the potty. And it is always on. There is nowhere to go nothing you can do to get away from it. It is just this constant streaming penetrating foolishness. Whether it is CNN; ESPN; TNN; or the Food Network the singular fact is that every broadcast is useless garbage. Garbage of the mind and heart.

When I travel. Which is rare. I do everything I can to try to get away from it. I sit in corners. I sit with my head down and my fingers in my ears. And still it penetrates. Sometimes if you're lucky in some place you can find the remote unattended and push the mute button. But it never lasts. Someone always wants to know what the Kardashians are doing today. I try to concentrate. I try to focus. I get my fingers in my ears my eyes on the page my head down. I concentrate on what I am reading on what I am thinking on what I am writing but I almost always fail. There will be some shift in the cadence of the presenter as they reiterate that the missing airliner is missing and it will break my train of thought. This is the thing that most irritates me: With the television on there is no space for thinking.

If I were a conspiracy theorist—which I am not—I could have a field day with this. This is more Orwellian than 1984; it is more coercive than the slogans of Animal Farm. We have achieved world dominance through the stealthy turning of every brain to mush. We have reduced the average attention span to 20 seconds. We have convinced the masses that the words coming from the television are important. This is perfect. No longer will we face the threat of the man who has learned to think for himself.

When I was a kid people smoked cigarettes where ever and whenever they pleased. In the car in the plane in the restaurant and definitely in the potty. Over the course of my lifetime however the dangers of second hand smoke have become so well known that legislatures everywhere have moved to ban indoor smoking. Today it is extremely rare at least in the United States to smell cigarette smoke in any public place. But what about second hand TV? Surely the overflow of televised inanity poses a greater threat to human health than cigarette smoke ever did. I mean smoke might kill you but television forces you to live forever with a splintered psyche. If you want to smoke in an airport today you are banished to a small filthy closet. Why not do the same for television? Anyone who really wants to be bludgeoned by foolishness can go sit in a sound-proofed cave.

On my way to the hotel I stopped for a deli sandwich and a six pack. In my room I ate the sandwich and drank a couple of beers. I called Michelle. We each described the contents of our day. We were like an old married couple. *Oh. That's so? Uh-huh.* It was OK though. It was nice to have someone to talk to. After a while I got into the bed with a book. I dozed off at about 10p but was awakened within the hour by the arrival of the Bovine family in the room above me. I listened to them rearrange the furniture until two in the morning. When they finally settled in for cud chewing in the shade of the juniper tree I was able to doze fitfully for a couple of hours. By five I was ready to be up. I felt bad but there was nothing to be done for it. I went to the lobby for a cup of lobby coffee and took a shower.

I went for an early morning walk. I ate a scone and drank another cup of coffee. I sat at my laptop and responded to a couple of emails. At 7:30a I put everything in my shoulder back and checked out. I walked to the head office. The Illium corporate headquarters. I got someone to let me in and wandered the halls for a while. I knew a few people so I stopped to say "hi" and shake a few hands. By nine I was in the design department waiting for Jenifer. And Beth. Beth I'd met before. But not her boss. Jenifer. They came in late. They were smiley and friendly. But not—I don't know—respectful. They acted like I was stupid. Like I was silly. Something. I ignored it mostly. But they were kind of a pain in the ass.

—Well. Don't you think that would be illegal?

—How? How illegal?

—You can't just steal someone else's art. Don't you think that would violate the copyright?

—I'm not suggesting that we steal anything.

And on and on. For a couple of hours. It's not like I'm new to the business. I know what I'm doing. And I don't expect a lot. Just help me get the thing through layout and design. Then we can all go do something else. Heck. I would do it myself if you didn't need some excuse for collecting a paycheck. Anyway. I was as polite as I could be. I really was. I even went with Jenifer to an early lunch. Which she spent looking at her phone.

The little turbo-prop from Vegas to Box Elder County was only half full—the front half. Naturally everybody picks a seat towards the front of the aircraft. That is what I had done and I had my best seat of the week: I was by myself and I was one row from the door. The door was closed the engines were running and I had my magazine open.

Suddenly the stewardess was standing beside me with a somewhat urgent look on her face.

—The Captain.

She said.

—He needs someone to move to the back row to help balance the aircraft. Do you mind moving back there? You can have the whole row to yourself.

I looked at her blankly. I tried to think about what she had just said. I looked over my shoulder at the two buddies wedged into the row behind me talking loudly about puking during spring break—each of them going at more than 250 lbs. I looked back at the stewardess. The plane was starting to taxi. I looked across the aisle at the well-endowed lady filling out the other seat (200 lbs?). I looked back at the stewardess.

—You want me to move to the back row?

—Could you please. It is for aircraft balance.

I thought about how better our balance might be if pete and repeat behind me moved to the back row but I decided not to say it.

—OK.

I stood up and grabbed my bag—the bag had one t-shirt one pair of cotton socks and one pair of boxer shorts in it. All of them dirty. I hitched up my pants so they didn't fall down and walked to the back of the bus. She was right. I had it all to myself.

On Thursday I returned to the office. At eight sharp Dustin came to the door.

—Oh man. You missed it.

—Uh.

—Yeah. A real uproar yesterday.

—Oh yeah.

—Shew. Man. It was hilarious. You know that girl they got answering phones?

—Um.

—You know that gal always showing off her . . . you know.

—I'm not sure. The temp?

—Yeah. What's her name? They got her in here to answer phones.

—I think she is a temp. Judy or something.

—Yeah. That's the one. Well anyway. You know she's got those fake ones?

He made a gesture with his hands.

—She does?

—Yeah. Of course man. You see how they're always so hard and full?

—Well.

—That isn't natural you know.

—I guess I never really . . .

—It's those cheap saline implants. They over inflate 'em. Install one size and inflate 'em up to the next size. It removes all the wrinkles.

—It does?

—Yeah. Well anyway. You see hers. They're definitely that cheap kind.

—OK.

—Anyway the problem with those cheap ones is that they can deflate. You go to bed with two and wake up with one. Know what I mean?

—Hard to imagine.

—Well. One of hers sprung a leak yesterday. Caused quite an uproar.

—How's that?

—She's kind of a high maintenance gal. You know. Sort of had a breakdown. Running around the office calling her plastic surgeon. Real loud.

—That's terrible.

—Well I guess the surgeon wanted a picture of the problem. Can you believe it?

—I guess.

—So she's asking people to take a picture of it. Of the deflated one. She is handing them her phone. You know with the camera.

—Oh.

—Wanting them to follow her into an empty office or the bathroom so she can pick up her shirt and have them take some pictures.

—Uh.

—Nobody would do it.

—That's good. I guess.

—The thing is. She doesn't really need 'em. She can't be more than 28. Early thirties max.

—Oh.

—You don't need 'em when you're young. You should wait until you've had your kids. Finished nursing.

—You should?

—Yeah. Like my first wife. She got 'em after we were done having kids. First pair was cheap. Those saline ones.

—They were?

—Yeah. They lasted five or eight years. One of them started leaking. So we shopped around. Finally went with the same guy.

—Oh.

—Paid a little more for the silicone. She used some of the money she inherited from her grandmother. I made up the difference.

—Yeah.

—I thought they came out pretty good. She wasn't happy with that second set though.

—Oh.

—Of course. She took 'em with her when we got divorced.

—I guess so.

Dustin laughed.

—My current wife is jealous.

—Oh yeah.

—She's seen pictures.

—Huh?

—You know. Digging through old pictures of my wife that I still have on my home computer. I don't know. Why does she do that?

—Yeah.

—Anyway. She keeps telling me that I have to buy some for her. She says that since I paid for my first wife's I should buy her some too. I keep telling her that I'm not doing that again. I lost all my money the first time. If she wants 'em she can pay for them herself.

—Uh. Huh.

—Shew. Man. You missed your chance.

—I did?

—Yeah. You could have been in here with young Judy yesterday taking pictures.

23

Here in front of him was a wild mallard—just arrived from the home
of the north wind. The creature brought within him an amplitude of
Northern knowledge. Glacial catastrophes, snowstorm episodes,
glittering auroral effects, Polaris in the zenith, Franklin underfoot,—
the category of his commonplaces was wonderful. But the bird, like
many other philosophers, seemed as he looked at the man to think
that a present moment of comfortable reality was worth a decade of
memories.

Thomas Hardy

   The last big task was the framing. A stick built house has a lot of sticks.
Breaking a stick built house requires breaking a lot of sticks. Actually. I try
not to do much breaking. Two by fours are worth something. If I can sell
them I sell them. If not I use them around my own place. Repairing sheds.
Building fences. Propping up foundations.
   Watch somebody frame a house. It isn't necessarily easy. Even a good
framer needs to put some time into it. Some thought. I mean. You have
to know where the windows are going to go. The doors. The closets. You
have to follow the directions. Or whatever. The map. The blueprint.
Things need to be square. They have to be plumb. Chalk lines and crap.
You can't hang a window if it doesn't fit the hole. You don't want your
doors to stick. You have to know where the interior walls are going to go.
Where is the bathroom going to go? You've got headers. Plates. Studs.
Which is which? You're going to have to hang sheetrock on one side and
siding on the other.
   Breaking it is much easier. It doesn't take a lot of thought. You don't

want to hit yourself in the head. In the eye. But otherwise it doesn't take a lot of planning. I'm pretty good at getting rid of the framing.

It was relatively late in the summer. Early autumn. I spent a couple of days swinging the hammer and running the saw. The saw. That is the other nice thing about breaking the framing. If you can't get it with the hammer you can always cut it and let it fall over.

In the end the biggest thing was the clean-up. Pulling nails. Sorting lumber. Piling it. Michelle helped. Helped relieve the boredom. We worked together. Talked a little.

The nice thing about going out for a walk in the woods or in a little wash somewhere is that all the people are gone. I mean. There are tens of millions of people in the western United States. It is crowded and noisy. But. In contrast to a hundred years ago or even fifty no one knows how to walk. Motors. Yeah. There are motors everywhere. At least two motors for every man woman and child. But if you can get to where the motorized access ends—and that can be difficult in some places—you can be alone. My rule of thumb is two tenths of a mile or 1000 feet. Some small percentage of people will walk that far. But almost no one will walk further than that. When I feel like being alone—which is most of the time—I drive to the end of the road and walk 1000 feet. Bingo.

The thing that is going to happen next. Is already happening. Drones. Personal drones. Recreational drones. It hasn't been a big problem yet. But it will soon affect every corner of the back country. They are cheap enough for just about anyone. Certainly cheaper than an ATV. Want a nice picture of that canyon? No need to walk up there. Just fly your drone. Run the video camera. In twenty minutes you'll have a movie of the whole place. You'll have a movie of me giving you the finger. I don't know. It's like the developers. They are everywhere. And there is no way to stop them. Pretty soon it will be the same with the droners. Everywhere. And no stopping them. You could shoot them down I guess. Morally that would be OK. More than OK. The right thing to do. Shoot the drone and shoot the droner too. But. Legally. No. I wouldn't like the legal chances of the shooter as against the droner.

One Saturday in the early autumn we were at the café. Talking about books. Mostly. Paintings too. I mean. What else?

—So what is your all-time favorite book?

—Well. The best piece of fiction ever written is A River Runs Through It. But I don't know.

—Don't know what?

—Well. It's only a hundred pages. It's not really a novel. Not really a short story either.

—A novella.

—Yeah. Whatever that is. And it is autobiographical. It is hard to tell how much of it is really fiction.

—OK.

—And the out-put was so small. McLean's publisher combined it with a couple of other short stories. They weren't horrible but nowhere near the quality of River. So. I don't know what you can say for it? For him? It was one hundred pages of absolute perfection. But there was nothing else.

—With all those qualifications it is hard to see how it is your favorite.

—Well. OK. You want my unqualified selection?

—Yeah. Your unqualified selection.

—A Farewell to Arms. Probably the finest piece of fine art in the world. Not counting Maynard Dixon's High in the Morning of course.

She laughed.

—I've never liked it. The ending is horrible.

—Dixon's? Yeah. I guess. It is tragic ending and all that. But three hundred pages of hard clean writing? It is hard to argue with that.

—Masculine writing.

—It is. Masculine writing. I guess that fits me. But how about you? What is your all-time favorite?

—I don't know. I'll put in a plug for the women. Cather.

—OK. Which?

—Archbishop maybe. Or Pioneers.

—Good enough.

—Marilynne Robinson.

—Yes. In a class by herself.

—And Wharton.

—What? No. That is horrible. Not Wharton. Age of Innocence? Awful. The worst thing I've ever read.

I was laughing. Michelle laughed too.

—What do you mean? She won the Pulitzer.

—I know. But. Her characters are so hateful. You can't possibly like anyone in that stupid story. Archer? Are you kidding? What an unpleasant boorish fool. By the end you are just hoping that he gets run over by a train.

We were both laughing.

—What about Thomas Hardy? Not a woman. Not an American. But more of a feminine style.

—Yeah. He's good. I like Hardy.

—Tess?

—Yeah. What?

—OK. She is a pretty lousy character too. Right? But at least she has the decency to throw herself into the mill pond.

Michelle was still laughing.

—Oh. Another horrible ending. You really are a heartless jerk. You only like the ones where the lady dies gruesomely at the end.

—Hey. I'm an equal opportunity hater. I was perfectly thrilled to see the deadbeat Damon drown himself too.

That afternoon I was splitting wood on the east side of my shed when a hulking old pickup rumbled to a stop. Kendall. He got out and gave a shout.

—How's that new saw?

—It's OK. No complaints yet.

He worked past the shed and stopped by my chopping block. Kendall. A twinkle in his eye. A smile on his face.

—Just thought I'd stop to see how you're doing with your wood. And that new saw.

—Oh. You know. It's going OK. I'm plugging away. How 'bout you?

—Shew. I gotta cut 14 or 15 cord this year.

—Holy crap. That's something. What's going on?

—Well. My sister. You know. She's got cancer. Her husband don't get around too good anymore either. Blind in one eye. I told 'em not to worry. Plus there's my old man. By the time I get four or five cords for each a them. Gotta cut that much for myself too.

He gave a smile. Like he almost relished it. Like it felt good to say 15 cord. Like he'd forgotten all about his surgery earlier in the year.

—Gonna get a new saw though.

—Y'are?

—Yeah. I got ten years outta that old Husky. I shoulda been able to get more. But I guess that's OK.

—What are you gonna get?

—I've got another Husky on layaway. But I like the Stihl. I'm wondering about that.

He pronounced it "steel." Some people say it "still." I don't know and I don't care. I simply enjoyed listing to the guy. Old Kendall. He was unique. The only person in America without a complaint. Content. Happy with who he was and what he had. Exceedingly unusual in this land of envy. And he didn't have much. He'd been laid off from his job. His wife was infirm. He was cutting wood and living on what? Social security?

—It'll probably take me 'til this time next year to pay for it.

He laughed. Shrugged. Looked me in the eye.

—How's things going on the house over there?

He meant the Ewell place. It was my turn to laugh.

—Not too good. It doesn't look like much does it?

—I've lived here more than thirty years. I've never seen someone take a house down. I've seen plenty of 'em put up. But I can't say I've ever seen that.

—Yeah. Probably stupid.

—Yeah. Probably.

He pronounced it "parbly." He laughed again. Looked me square in the face. His eyes were friendly.

—Well. I best be getting over to home before the wife starts shouting. Have a good week.

—You too.

The way the whole probate drama worked out was somewhat anti-climactic. I got a large envelope in the mail. It contained my offer for the house with West's signature. A contract. The rest of it was from the title company. Everything we needed for closing. West had signed it all.

I called him to ask what had happened. He was busy. Didn't want to talk.

—The judge approved it.

—What ever happened with the probate business?

—It was his view that—under the circumstances—it was a low risk transaction. But we can't give you a general warrantee deed.

—OK.

—I've talked with the title company. They're going to issue a special warrantee deed. It's the best we can do. We'll pay for title insurance.

—Alright. Well.

—That's about it. Our part is done. It is closed as far as we're concerned.

—I see your signature on everything.

—Yeah. Just call the title company. Go over there and sign. It will be a done deal.

—Do I need to bring any money?

It was a joke. But West didn't laugh. Like I said he seemed to be in a hurry.

—It was good working with you.

—Yeah. You too.

That was the last time I spoke with him. I went to the title company the next day and signed the closing documents. At that point the house was mine. At this point the property is mine but the house is mostly gone.

The next day I went to church with Michelle. It was the first time. And not the last either. I mean. It was awful. It really was. But I was in church with my girlfriend. So I was willing to put up with a little more than usual. Actually. For someone as grumpy as me the place wasn't so bad.

It was old. I mean everything was old. The building. The pews. The organist. The minister. The congregation. I don't know. It was probably dying. A dying community. Few if any young families. The hope of the growing church.

They weren't attracting the flip-flop wearers. The tattoo people. They weren't seeker sensitive. They had no band. They didn't have the Jefferson Airplane on the stage. Most of them probably didn't even have a smart phone. I heard only a single cell phone call come through during the entire service. One. Can you imagine? This was a disconnected crowd.

The hymns were old. Old and boring. The homily was just as bad. It didn't need to be. The gospel lesson was from Matthew: *Then saith he to his servants, The wedding is ready, but they which were bidden were not worthy. Go ye therefore into the highways, and as many as ye shall find, bid to the marriage. So those servants went out into the highways, and gathered together all as many as they found, both bad and good: and the wedding was furnished with guests.* I almost laughed. It was the vision of Mrs. Turpin. But instead of making the connection— instead of making any connection—all we got was a straight explanation of the parable. Jesus telling the Pharisees how they'd been rejected. It was dull. It was boring. It really was. At least there was no skit.

I was sitting there with Michelle. So I wasn't going to get up and go. No matter how dull. We got to the *Te Deum*. Chanted it. Chanted the *Te Deum*. It wasn't dull. It was beautiful. Not often do you chant the *Te Deum*. Not anymore. I liked it quite a bit.

On the way out Michelle introduced me to the minister. Standing at the back door. Everyone on the way to coffee hour. The pastor. Richard.

—This is John.

—Hey John. Glad you could join us today.

—Yeah. Thanks.

—We've got coffee. And one of the ladies made cupcakes. It's Elsa Jansen's birthday today.

—Oh. Sounds good.

—Well. Hope to see you again next week. It was great to have you.

—Thanks.

I steered Michelle to the door. There was no way I was having cupcakes with Elsa. I could hear Richard. Behind us. Saying goodbye.

—It was good to meet you. Jim.

At least he didn't call me buddy.

24

I hired Bobby to do the earth work. We agreed that we'd leave the sewer line in the ground. It was deep enough that I'd never hit it with a shovel. Or even a backhoe. But the water line and the gas line were within five feet of the surface. With both of them disconnected and the meters removed Bobby dug a trench and we pulled all the pipe between the slab and the street. He broke it up with his tracks and I stacked it out of the way to be recycled. Bobby filled and packed the trenches and we turned our attention to the slab.

Bobby shut down his machine and climbed stiffly to the ground. He came over to where I was standing. I was holding a shovel and had one foot on the slab.

—One thing we could do. We could drill it and blast it.

—You mean dynamite?

—Sure. It would save a lot of cleanup. We could put enough powder in it to get rid of most of it.

—Where would it go?

He laughed.

—All over the neighborhood.

Now I knew that he was joking. Which was something of a relief.

—Blast it to kingdom come huh?

—Yeah. Less to haul away.

—Would it bother the neighbors?

—There might be some breakage.

Bobby's phone rang. He pulled it out. An iphone. He talked on it. He put it away. Just like that. Happens all the time. He acted like a twenty-year-old punk. A regular hipster. Getting a call on the mobile. Never mind that he'd been born before the depression.

—One time. Up in Idaho. Must have been the nineteen fifties. Yeah.

After the war anyway. I was working for a guy. Construction. You know. We were supposed to be building a foundation on this building in town. I don't know. Idaho Falls? Pokie? Twin? I can't remember. Anyway. We dug down for the foundation and encountered this bed rock. You know. Basalt or something. Hard. Volcanic. Couldn't dig through it or around it or anything.

—Yeah.

—So this guy. Greek guy. Owned the construction company. He told me to blast it. Those old Greeks were tough sons a bitches. He didn't care. He wanted it gone. I was his blaster. Back then they called us powder monkeys. Anyway I was the powder monkey. Except I really didn't know what I was doing. I got the job because I'd been an engineering technician for six months with another construction company. Sure I'd helped blow a couple of things but I never had a lot of experience. I'd certainly never blasted a piece of bedrock like this one.

—How'd it go?

—Well. Let's just say I used too much powder. It got rid of the problem with the foundation but it caused a few others.

—Injure some people?

—Actually no. It was lucky. We did it at night when no one was on the street. Probably woke up a few folks though. The worst thing was just the damage to the adjoining building. All the windows were blown out and the wall was cracked. Windows were gone all over town.

—Wow. What happened?

—Well. People were pretty angry. By the next morning they were all but ready to lynch me and this Greek guy—especially him. He agreed to fix everything though and they calmed down a little bit. He chewed me out and sent me to another job. He didn't fire me. Just sent me down to Salt Lake City to work on another project. I was glad enough to get out of there.

—What ever happened to him?

—People didn't necessarily like Greeks back then and somebody might have wanted to take a shot at him. But he was tough. Boy oh boy. Iron willed and relentless. He actually carried a six-shot revolver in his pocket like an old time cowboy. Would have used it too. You wanted to get a shot at him you better do it in the dark and from the back. Anyway along with all that he was honest and fair. He put his construction crew right to work making repairs all over town.

Jerry saw me and came around the fence. He wanted to tell me about his buddy who worked for Goldman Saks. Something. It was hard to hear him. Over the leaf blower. Jerry had a guy in his yard. Two of them. Mowing edging raking. Mexicans. You know. He had a yard service. He had hired a yard service. One of the guys was cleaning the sidewalk and driveway with a leaf blower. A cloud of blue smoke billowed. It was loud as hell. Jerry was yelling so I could hear him. Yelling to be heard over the leaf blower.

Now. It is none of my business. But I know that Jerry and Danielle each have a gym membership. They pay for a gym membership. At the same time they pay a couple of Mexican guys to run the power mower and the leaf blower. It seems as though they are missing an opportunity. They could cancel both the yard guys and the gym guys and buy a rake. A clean yard and fit body for the price of a rake. You ever see what a lot of raking does to your shoulders? Danielle would look good after two hours of raking.

Anyway. I know it is crazy. And it isn't just Jerry and Danielle. They are merely doing what everybody else does. You pay for a labor saving device and then pay for the privilege of laboring at the gym. People want to ride the mower and blow the leaves. But they are fat. So they want to go to the gym too. Have you ever seen someone who splits his own wood and mows his own lawn? He is not fat. He doesn't pay to go to the gym.

I don't know what I'm talking about. I have never even been to a gym. Not since I played intramural basketball at college. But it does make me wonder. I see it all the time. Guy makes a New Year's resolution to lose 40 pounds. Buys a fancy bike. A bunch of lycra. A weight set. I don't know. A Nordic Track. Something. Pretty soon you can see it sitting on the patio with bird shit on the seat. When the grass starts growing in the yard the guy goes back and forth on his riding mower. He is still 40 pounds overweight.

The next week. At our dive café. Saturday morning. She asked me about the church.
—Can you stand it?
—Stand what?
—Richard and the rest of the Lutherans.
—You know. It was OK. But the best part was you.
—Me?
—Yeah. I liked being with you.
—OK. So you can tolerate the church?
—I can tolerate it. And I really admire you.
She laughed.
—Are you trying to get a date?
—I've just been thinking about you.
—About me?
—Yeah. You're like Dean Moriarty's perfect woman.
—Dean Moriarty?

—Yeah.

—I hope you don't admire Dean Moriarty.

—I don't admire his treatment of his women.

—Women?

—I don't admire his treatment of his women; and I wouldn't treat my woman that way.

—Good. But what about his perfect woman?

—Remember that time in San Francisco when he and Sal went home with that guy Walter after a night of getting their kicks in all the jazz bars?

—Vaguely.

—Well. It's dawn and the three of them come in and disturb Walter's wife. Climb all over the bedroom plugging in lights. And then settle in to drink beer. At six or seven in the morning. The wife just smiles.

—You admire women like that?

—No. Yes. I mean. I shouldn't have started this. I'm digging a deep one here. When Dean and Sal finally leave the apartment Dean proclaims that Walter's wife is the perfect woman. Or a great woman. Or his favorite woman. Something like that.

—Because she just let the three of them walk all over her?

—Oh. Lord. I was trying to give you a compliment. I can see I really screwed this up. Dean just really admires that woman. He tells Sal that he digs her positive attitude. She didn't complain. Didn't whine. She just let her husband have a couple of people over for some beers. You know. She was just a really kind and patient person. Like you.

—OK. Mister. You should stick to criticizing people. You're terrible at giving complements.

I laughed.

—I know. That was stupid.

—But I really like that book.

—On the Road? You do?

—Yeah.

—Wow. I'm surprised. It isn't a very nice book in a lot of ways.

—I know.

—I mean. There is a lot of joy in the way Dean (and Sal) experience the newness and beauty of what they see—what they drive through at 100 MPH. But the essential story is one of masculine self-gratification.

—I know. But it is just so beautifully written.

—That's funny.

—What?

—Kerouac is known for his role in the movement. Beat. Hippy. Hipster. Whatever. But I'm not sure I've ever heard anybody talk about his writing.

—He is really a good writer.

—I agree. He is an inventive and energetic writer.

—But for all that his story is about men without self-control his writing is controlled. It is exuberant but not sloppy. He knew what he was doing.

—Yass. Yass.

She laughed.

—One of my favorite things. Something that always sticks in my mind. Is Kerouac's description of Dean in full cry. Getting his kicks. In. I think. Denver. It is towards the end. It just sticks in my mind: *Dean became frantically and demoniacally and seraphically drunk.*

I laughed.

—Brilliant. Demoniacally and seraphically.

—And to think. He couldn't find a publisher because he was too experimental. It took six or eight years.

—For what?

—From when he wrote it until when it was finally published.

25

That's the whole trouble. You can't ever find a place that's nice and peaceful because there isn't any. You may think there is, but once you get there, when you're not looking, somebody'll sneak up and write "Fuck you" right under your nose. Try it sometime.

J.D. Salinger

Bobby took the slab with him when he left. In a dump truck. In a thousand pieces.

When he was done there was plenty of debris left over. I spent a couple of weeks raking through the dirt and grass. I picked out the concrete. I picked the plastic. The nails.

I brought over the old rototiller. The bull. It may have been built in the 1950s. It must have weighed a thousand pounds. I'd paid $50 for it ten years ago. At a yard sale. It was self-propelled. It was impossible. It was a rodeo event. I'm not necessarily a weakling. But riding the bull took all that I had. I got it revving. Put it in gear. And hung on. It put up a rooster tail of dirt. It was November. I was working in a T-shirt. I was sweating. I got it turned and went back. And forth. Back and forth.

When it was done it looked pretty good. Smooth. Dirt. Smooth dirt. I put the bull away. I was exhausted. The wind blew. I was wet with sweat. I was freezing. I went in my house. Put on a fresh T-shirt. Put on a sweatshirt. Put on a hat. Grabbed a bottle of wine.

I went back over to the Ewell house. The Ewell lot. I propped the wine on a pile of lumber. I opened the bottle. I looked across the lot at the wall separating it from Jerry and Danielle's mansion. I picked up the bottle and drank one third of it.

There were no chickens. There were no dogs. There were no ATVs. There were no pick-up trucks. There were no satellite dishes. There were no bikes. There were no lawn mowers. There was no trash.

Somebody roared past on the street. Big diesel truck. Thump thump thump. Must have been some gangsters huh? Out of the corner of my eye I saw something come out the window. Trash. But I ignored it. I'm not seeing you. I'm not hearing you.

Under my breath I said Fuck all y'all.

It looked good. It really did. The blue plastic piece of shit house was gone. I was almost happy. But not quite. I have that knack. I can ruin anything. I can turn any good situation into a reason to feel bad.

This is the thing. You can maybe change the situation but you can't change yourself. Oh I know. You can go to church. Go to the gym. Go to the therapist. But. Hell. At the end of the day you're stuck with yourself.

Noise and trash irritate me. They always have and always will. You get rid of one piece of trash and someone throws another at you. If you can't deal with that you're always going to be angry. Right then. I was kind of angry. I picked up the wine and went home.

Michelle's parents came to town. They wanted to see her of course. But there was also some desire—evidently—to meet me. She must have told them that she was with someone.

They arrived late on a Thursday afternoon. I drove Michelle to the airport. We parked in the garage. Short term. We walked to the terminal. Looked on the monitor for the gate. She didn't say anything. I didn't either.

The flight was on time. C concourse. We went to the security barrier. Took up a position where we could look for them coming out. There were other people waiting too. Michelle was quiet. We were holding hands.

—I don't think you'll like them.

I laughed. I looked at her. I pulled her back a few steps. Found a place against the wall. I squatted down. My back against the wall. I pulled her down. We squatted together. I put my hand on her knee.

—What is going on?

—My parents are not easy to be with. I don't think you'll like them. I wish they weren't coming. It is stressing me out.

—I can get along with just about anyone. Don't worry about it.

—I don't think that is true.

—What?

—That you can get along with just about anyone.

I laughed.

—OK. But I'm not going to have a problem with your parents. I'm looking forward to meeting them. It will be fine. And it is only for a couple of days.

—OK. But.

She put her head on my shoulder.

—But what?

—I want you to like me after they are gone.

—I like you plenty. Don't worry about it.

She pulled my face around and kissed me. We stood up. I smiled at her. We stepped forward. She squeezed my hand.

—That's them.

The thing—I guess—about most big companies is that no one really wants to work. You go there every day. But mostly everyone is trying to avoid the hard work. The work that hurts. The work that forces you to sit and struggle. The work that makes you sweat blood. The work that leaves you exhausted.

It can't be like this everywhere. Probably there are places where people like to work. Probably there are places where people have to work. But big companies. And agencies. People can maneuver into comfortable sinecures. Positions where no one really pushes them. And where there are always plenty of excuses. Distractions. I've got something else to do right now. Important meetings. And webinars. Rewriting policies. Policies about how to conduct webinars.

Not me. Hey. I'm not trying to toot my own horn. This is not a moral judgment. In fact it is—if anything—a character flaw. But I'd rather work. I prefer work. I really do. I like to work. When I go to work I want to work. Unfortunately. I spend most of my working time trying to fend off the distractions. Would you like to join the Office Safety Committee? No. In fact. I really wouldn't. I have work to do. And I want to do it. Joining the book police is nothing but a distraction.

On the Friday after our airport meeting Michelle didn't come to work. Didn't come to the office. She took the day off to show her parents around the area. Her absence was something of a relief. It removed my biggest distraction. Don't get me wrong. I liked just about everything about her. I enjoyed seeing her every day. But her presence was a distraction. It was one more thing that impacted my ability to concentrate. Without her in the office I looked forward to a ten hour marathon of work. Head down. World at bay. Work. Thinking. Concentrating. Banging on it.

By 9:30 Dustin was in the chair.

—Flew back from headquarters yesterday.

—Yeah. I heard you were going out there.

—Had to meet with Mahoney.

—Planning a big campaign?

—Yeah. Want to put out a lot of our best material in an e-reader format. Anyway. Heard some rumors about you.

—Me?

—Yeah.

—Rumors?

—Yeah.

—What do you mean?

—Well some of those gals in design think you were pretty rude with the cover of that biography.

—Are you kidding?

—Nope. Said you weren't a team player. Kind of a renegade. All that. You know.

—Lord. I went there to work with them. Smiled. Groveled. Lurked around the office all day. I even went to lunch with that lady Jenifer. We talked all through it. They were going to take care of everything for me. Six weeks went by. I emailed. I called. I never heard a thing from them. We needed to move. So I did it myself.

—Hey. I'm not saying anything.

—You would think they'd be happy. I did their job for them. Saved them some time. Gave them some extra time for gossiping.

—Yeah. A lot of that over there.

—Why don't they just shut up? It's not hurting them. They didn't do it so I did. What does that matter to them?

—Hey. I'm just the messenger.

No. Dustin wasn't the messenger. He was the busybody. Nobody likes a busybody I guess. But a gossiper is worse. Somebody who talks crap behind your back. Now that really irritates me. So much for a day without distractions. I was already side tracked and it wasn't even ten in the morning.

Michelle and her parents invited me out to dinner on Saturday evening. They were staying at the Hampton Inn near the University. They wanted to eat at the Chili's next door to the motel. Sure. Whatever. I drove my truck and stopped for Michelle. We met them there.

There were four of us in the booth. I was sitting across from Michelle's father. Arthur. Art. They were talkers. The parents. Were talkers. Non-stop. Talking over each other. Talking to me; to Michelle. Interrupting each other. Arguing. Talking. Michelle broke in occasionally. I didn't. I sat and listened. Or tried to. Art ordered a glass of wine. Evidently his second or third of the afternoon. Urged me to join him. Which I did. When the food came the rate of talking slowed. But didn't stop. Talk about their neighbors. About their other kids. About their various illnesses and infirmities. About where they had traveled. Where they were planning to travel. At no point did they ask me anything about myself. Which was just as well. But what was the point in travelling to meet me? What they knew about me was my name and where I worked. But they'd known that before leaving home.

Art's next glass of wine came. The food was running out and that gave him a fresh opportunity to talk. Now it was about politics.

—It's all calculated to gain further control over people. I tell you. That guy they got in there now. A communist. A Maoist. Arrogant. He's not going to step down when his term ends. You mark my words. He is gathering cadres to keep him in power. Trampling the constitution. There needs to be a revolution. I'm sorry to say that. But I'll be fine when it comes. Guy I know says he can get me an AK-47. Everybody in my neighborhood will have one. When those communist bastards—those terrorists—come to take control we'll be ready.

It almost made me laugh. I remember when the other guy was in charge. Friends from the other side of the divide swore that he was a Nazi. Hitler reborn. Gathering brown shirts to himself. Was not going to step down. Would not go peacefully. We'd need a revolution.

It is amazing how many Americans get into that silliness. If the other guy wins office they decide to start buying ammunition. Meanwhile nothing changes. The next campaign begins immediately. And no one turns out to be planning to overstay their term. I guess they hear that stuff on TV. Fucking TV.

Anyway. It irritates me. From the right and from the left. Highly irritating. It is pure foolishness. Well. This irritation caused me to make a mistake.

—Actually I don't think he is a communist. He is more of a statist.

It might have been the only thing I said all night. It interrupted the monologue. Art stared at me for a long second. Then he exploded. Glaring and stabbing his finger at me. Shouting.

—It may already be too late. This whole thing has been calculated from the start. The brain washing. The whole propaganda machine. To take power and install a communist government. And we aren't going to stand for it. People are going to rise up. Blood is going to be spilled. It is happening right now.

Michelle's mother tried to intervene. Anne. Anne pulled on his arm. Michelle leaned across me and called his name. He would not be deterred or distracted. But they got some help the form of our cute young waitress.

—Is anyone interested in dessert?

Art's face changed. He sat back. Relaxed. Smiled at the waitress. Asked for the dessert menu. Made a comment about how the boys must all be after her. Art was from the generation that thought nothing of flirting with the waitress. OK. I don't know if it has to do with his generation.

Maybe he was just that kind of guy.

—I'm treating tonight. Have anything you like.

—Oh. No thanks. I need to get going here in a few minutes.

—That's right. Dad. John needs to get out of here at a reasonable hour tonight. We should be going soon.

The waitress returned with a plate of sample desserts. Art began to study them. I stood up. Anne started in on me.

—Oh. John. It has been so good to see you. Please. Can't you stay for dessert.

—Thanks Anne. Thanks for the invite. No. I really should be going.

Michelle stood.

—We can run you home dear. It's no problem. Why don't you stay and have some dissert with your Dad.

—Oh. I ate so much. I couldn't. I'm really full Mom. I'll plan to see you both in the morning.

—Well. OK.

I reached over to shake her hand. Anne's hand. Art. Who had been ignoring us—turning the dessert plate back and forth—suddenly looked up. He put out his hand. I shook it briefly. I turned for the door. I heard Michelle tell him goodbye and a few seconds later I felt her behind me. Her hand groping for mine. I walked fast. I pulled her along. I heard the door of the restaurant close behind us.

—That was insane.

—I'm sorry.

—What was that all about?

—He is just like that. Always has been.

—Was it me? Was he out to get me?

—No. He does it to everybody.

—He does? What is wrong with him?

—I knew you wouldn't like them.

—You say it as though I had a choice. Does anyone like them?

—I don't know. They've got some old cronies they hang around with.

—You're not like them. Like him. Are you?

—I'm not. I'm really not.

—But where did you come from? These are your parents.

—I wasn't raised by them.

—You weren't?

—They were too busy. Working all the time. I had an older sister who was kind of in trouble. I had an older brother with a learning disability. They didn't have time for me. I grew up alone. Reading. I was raised by books.

We got to the passenger door of my truck. I opened it and helped her in. I looked at her. There were tears in her eyes. I pushed her in.

—Sit in the middle.

I closed the door. I went around to the other side. I got in and started the truck. She was sitting next to me. I put the truck in gear and my arm around her shoulders. We idled out of the parking lot.

—Where do you want to go?

—Can I stay with you?

—You were raised by books?

—Yeah.

—Then you can stay with me.

26

His eyes were red and sleepless: he seemed to [be] one of those who
are quite unsuited to loneliness. There were no books to be seen
except a little shelf with his breviary and a few religious tracts. He
was a man without resources.

Graham Greene

On the Sunday after Thanksgiving Richard invited his congregation to
remain after the benediction for an additional ceremony. Brief. An
additional brief ceremony. For those who were interested. Only for those
with time and interest. The others were welcome to go to the fellowship
hall for coffee. Cake would be served in the hall at the conclusion of the
additional ceremony. The additional brief ceremony.

I stayed. I stood with Michelle at the altar. Alone. We were alone at
the altar. Just the two of us.

—Wilt thou have this woman to be thy wife and wilt thou pledge they
troth to her, in all love and honor, in all duty and service, in all faith and
tenderness, to live with her, and cherish her, according to the ordinance of
God, in the holy bond of marriage?

—I will.

—Wilt thou have this woman to be thy wife and wilt thou pledge they
troth to her, in all love and honor, in all duty and service, in all faith and
tenderness, to live with her, and cherish her, according to the ordinance of
God, in the holy bond of marriage?

—I will.

Most of the congregation waited—kept their seats. It took ten or fifteen
minutes. Then we all went out to the fellowship hall. The cake was white.

It was lettered with our names. John. Michelle. We cut and served it. With coffee. Cake and coffee. Wedding cake. Coffee hour. In the fellowship hall.

The additional ceremony had not been announced. Had not been in the bulletin. As a result there were no gifts. This was a disappointment to some. But not to me. I didn't want it. Didn't want them. No gifts.

But we stood for a long time. Holding hands. Receiving congratulations. And best wishes. I knew few of them by name. Old people. A bunch of old people in that church. Old church. Dull. Boring. Old. The building was old. The organ was old. But they loved us that day. They loved us. They loved us. Old men. Hardly recognized. Took my hand. Held it. Looked me in the eye. Old ladies. Pulling me down. Tears on their cheeks. Arms around my neck. Whispering in my ear.

—D'ja get a prenup?

—A what?

—You know. An agreement. A prenuptial agreement. You gotta have one of those.

—Well actually.

—When I divorced my first wife. I had to give her half of everything I'd worked for. You add it all up and then you write a check. It makes you think.

—Yeah.

I prefer to keep my private business to myself. I don't generally talk about my marital or financial status. Especially around the office. But I'd recently married a co-worker from that same office so it was a little hard to keep it completely quiet. Michelle had moved into my house. We were commuting together. We were each wearing a ring. It was probably obvious that something was going on even without talking about it. And there had been talk. I don't mean vicious gossip or anything. I just mean that there is always plenty of chit-chat around the building and that kind of news gets around. Eventually it got to Dustin. He came in to congratulate me. Or advise me. Or talk at me.

—When my second wife and I got together I wrote it all up. Got it formalized too. You don't do it to hurt the person but you just never know what kind of baggage they might be carrying. Usually by the time you get to that second or third marriage people are carrying a lot of baggage.

—Yeah.

—I mean we've worked through most of it. But it was exhausting at first. She was—how to put it nicely?—not exactly truthful with me about her financial situation.

—Uh-huh.

—When we were dating she had a college degree, a good job, and money in the bank. I had no reason to doubt her but we did rush into it pretty quick. There were a lot of things I didn't know.

—Yeah.

—Like the student loan debt. She had defaulted on twenty grand or so and they wanted their money. Even worse she'd never finished the degree. I got my hands on her transcripts. "Cs" "Ds" and incompletes. She'd basically flunked out.

—Wow.

—Yeah. Then there was the IRS. She'd quit filing her taxes eight or ten years previously. Wouldn't admit it of course. Until I got the IRS on the phone. She swears he is lying. But the IRS guy doesn't give a shit. Obviously he's telling me the truth.

—Did she owe a lot?

—The funny thing is that she wasn't earning very much—had a pretty crappy job actually—so she could have had a refund every year. By not filing she was leaving the refund on the table. Stupid. Pure laziness.

—Yeah.

—I made her file all the back taxes. It wasn't easy. I mean we almost separated right there. Maybe we should have. But we got it done. Got three years of refunds and used it to pay down the student loan debt.

—Well that's good.

—And that wasn't all. It went on and on. I think we've finally worked through it. But she was living pretty wild before we got together. Irresponsible you know. By far the biggest surprise was the arrest warrant.

—Arrest warrant?

—She was kind of a bad driver. But she thought she could ignore the violations. After a few unpaid tickets there was a warrant out for her. We were already married. She was on her way home from visiting her sister. Not far from town. Cop pulled her over for speeding. Nothing egregious. The guy was just hunting for something. Well. He discovered that there was a pretty big warrant out for her. Took her straight to the county jail. First I know about the whole business is when I had to go bail her out. Cost me a couple thousand bucks.

—Holy cow.

—Yeah. Like I say you never know about this stuff. Gotta protect yourself. Protect your assets.

—Yeah.

—We've got a joint account now. We both put money into it. Even steven. But anything else is mine. Money I make over and above our monthly split I spend how I like. She complains sometimes. But I just say "Hey I had this job and these hobbies before you got here and I'll have them when you're gone." That shuts her up.

—I'll bet.

—The house too. I'm not going through that again. It was mine when I met her and it will be mine when she's gone. I told her she could buy-in. Give me the cash. But she didn't have it. I went to a lawyer. And she signed. So she knows I'm keeping the house.

—Sounds kind of adversarial.

—Naw. We're through with all that. Things are OK. We've got pretty good agreements. She knows she is better off with me than she was before.

—Financially anyway.

—What? Yeah. So you better do the same.

—Uh-huh.

—I know. I know. You're in the puppy love stage. And all that. But let me tell you. It doesn't last. And you gotta defend your assets.

—But what is it for? The novel. What does it do?

I was at the table in my house. I was sitting across from the woman from whom I needed to defend my assets. She had made me dinner. Using her own assets. I'd eaten her dinner and she'd drunk my wine. We were sharing assets—and talking about books.

—I don't know. Stories. Partly.

—Yeah. The best of them are good stories. (The worst of them are ideological screeds disguised as stories.) But are they true stories?

—You mean did they actually happen? Or are they telling what may be true to the writer?

—Exactly. They are telling—in my view—about the human condition. About something that is true of the human condition.

—Using a story to do it.

—Yeah. But why use a story? Why not an essay? People are this way.

—How boring.

—Yeah. Besides can you really get at it in an essay? Flannery O'Connor was once asked to explain her meaning in a nutshell. She supposedly replied—and this may be apocrypha—that if she could explain it in a nutshell she wouldn't need to write the story.

—But what about all those novels out there that are purely stories? I mean people don't pick up—who?—James Patterson or Judy Blume to try to understand the human condition.

—Yeah. I don't know. I'm not sure I've ever looked at any of those. But. How about if I give a different answer now?

—What?

—I think the story—when it seems like just a story—can help us put the world right. I mean. We can't control the world. And it is mostly a mess. But we can put things right in the story. I don't know. I'm thinking out loud. Take the best of them: I really like Smith's Gorky Park. Wouldn't the world be a better place if it really did have a Russian cop like Arkady

Renko? It is just a story. Sure. But wouldn't the world be right if Renko were running it?

—Yeah.

—Or. Maybe? Just putting our own world right? Like Wallace Stegner. He is supposed to have written Big Rock Candy Mountain as a way to purge his own heart of the memory of his father. It is fiction—sure—but it is a way to tell one's own story so as to fix one's own world.

—I guess we should all try it.

—Probably we should.

27

Is there anywhere on your place where a man can walk—walk a long way, off the roads, in the woods? Is there any place where a man can shoot a .22?

Bernard DeVoto

Because the Ewell property adjoined mine I could afford to do a little irrigating. I decided to try a small orchard. Early in the spring I tilled and picked trash. It is amazing how much tiny debris is left over from house breaking. Nails. Broken concrete. Plastic. Especially plastic. Plastic pieces by the million. I tilled. I raked. I picked. When I was ready I organized three rows and dug five holes in each row. I tried to space it so that each hole was twenty to twenty five feet from any other hole.

I went to the nursery and bought fifteen potted apple trees. Jonathan. Winesap. Yellow delicious. They were about six feet tall and had no leaves. I put one in each hole. Spread some steer manure. And watered them in. I mulched the whole grid with bark that I picked up from the county fairgrounds.

Michelle came out to watch on the afternoon that I planted the last of them. It was dusk. The days were still short. Late winter. The air was still. It was cold. But not bitter. I was working in a sweatshirt.

—How about raspberries?

—How about them?

—May I have some?

—Are you asking me to plant a raspberry patch for you?

—Yes. I know you're busy.

—You're right. I'm busy. I'm not going to do it today. But. Honestly.

You can have anything you want. You say what and where. I'll dig it for you.

—Really?

—Of course. What do you think? I'm here for you. And I'm a hell of a good shoveler.

—You're good at a lot of things.

—I am?

She came up. I could feel her cold against me. I was warm. She put frigid hands inside my shirt. A cold cheek against mine.

—You are.

Living together was cost effective. We had more money. Together. Not paying extra rent somewhere. Not paying for two sets of utilities. Better rates on our auto insurance. We were DINKs. Double income no kids. Four paychecks each month—two for me two for her. We talked about what to do with it.

—If you were queen? No obstacles.

—Oh. I don't know. That bathroom. Off the kitchen hall. It could be. I mean. The vanity is pretty crumby. But this is your house. I don't want to.

—No it isn't. It is your house too. Our house. I don't care. We're just talking. You want that bathroom renovated?

—I do.

—OK. What else?

—I don't know. I mean. It would be great to take a trip sometime or something. I've never been to Yellowstone.

I laughed.

—What?

—See. I feel so happy with you.

—What?

—You didn't say Mercedes. You don't want a Mercedes. A new town house. A Gucci handbag. A bunch of shit.

—Well. I'm not going to turn shit down. But. No. I guess I don't really think about that stuff.

—OK. You've said bathroom renovation. A trip to Yellowstone. What else?

She laughed.

—This is stupid.

—What?

—I've always wanted a stationary bicycle. Or even one of those trainers where you ride your actual bike on a sort-of indoor treadmill. It would be great to ride every day. You know. Just to keep in shape. But it can be hard to get out on the road sometimes. Rain. Snow. You know.

I laughed again.

—You want an indoor bicycle trainer?

—I do.

—And that is it? Your third wish.

—I guess so.

I got up from where I was on the floor and went to lay on her. She was on the sofa and she moved to let me. Lay on her. Full length. She was under me. I sucked on her neck. She laughed. I got up.

—Your turn.

—Yeah.

—Really. If you were king.

—Yeah.

—Come on.

—You probably aren't going to like this.

—Let me guess. You want to buy another house?

—The whole block.

—The whole block?

—The whole block. It will never happen. But think about it. Right now we need only Jerry and Danielle's place to finish this side.

—What's it worth?

—Yeah. Good question. What's it worth? It is worth what someone is willing to pay I guess. He told me that they paid two ten.

—Wow.

—I know. Not for me. Not for us. Now. If we could get it for a hundred. I'd be interested.

—How? They're not going to sell for a hundred.

—Of course not. We have to wait for them to default. I got the Ewell house from the bankruptcy court. I'm keeping my fingers crossed.

—How many other properties are there? On the block I mean?

—Four or five. I don't know. There is the pretty nice brick place on the back side from Jerry and Danielle. The corner lot beside that one is vacant. Then there is that run down place with the camper van that never seems to move. And then there is that guy Ron around on this other side. Maybe it's just four.

—Still.

—Yeah. Still is right. It's not going to happen. But wouldn't it be great. We'd have about five acres. All the trash and crappy houses and yappy dogs cleared out.

—What would we do?

—Build a big fence. Plant a lot of trees. Live in the woods behind our fence.

—Like Eden.

—Like Eden.

EPILOGUE

Rosewater said an interesting thing to Billy one time about a book that wasn't science fiction. He said that everything there was to know about life was in *The Brothers Karamazov*, by Feodor Dostoevsky. "But that isn't enough anymore," said Rosewater.

Kurt Vonnegut, Jr.

It had been a long day. A lot of interruptions. Phone calls. People stopping in. Needing something right away. Hard to concentrate. Hard to finish anything. Now it was late. Five-ish. It was a Friday in the spring. Pretty nice weather. The office was clearing out nicely. There were some over achievers who stayed late most nights. But usually Friday wasn't too bad. Mostly people cleared out by five. I wanted to go too. But I had a proposal to finish. I'd promised it to the director. And it was close. Thirty minutes. Thirty minutes without an interruption should do it. I had to put a few more numbers in the budget spreadsheet and then add the budget numbers to the final proposal. Close. It was close. My head was down. I was banging furiously on the keyboard. I felt someone come and stop at the office door. I didn't look up. Hoping they would take the hint. Of course not.

—Big doings in your neck of the woods.

I glanced up. It was Dustin. I looked down. Kept typing.

—Uh-huh.

—Did you see that on KRRC last night?

—Naw. I don't. Um.

I kept my head down. My typing was slow. I'm not really that great with numbers. I have to concentrate.

—That local reporter. What's her name? Sheila. Sheila Wilson. Something like that. Anyway she did that big report on the fly-in-fly-out development.

—Uh-huh.

—Up there near you. New neighbors for you. Probably millionaires.

I gave up on the budget. Sat back. Looked up. Dustin was lounging comfortably in the doorway. Oblivious. What proposal? Does anyone write proposals anymore?

—Where is that?

—You know. Just there adjacent to the freeway. In the valley. They had it on the news. Great opportunity for Box Elder County. Big new development. They're going to build a new freeway ramp for it.

—Who is going to build a new freeway ramp?

—The developers. Local group got together to purchase the property. Had a some financial support from some big California company too. Headed by that guy Young. What's his name? Vice president of the builders association. Young somebody.

—Steve?

—Yeah. Steve Young. Young. They had the guy on the news program last night. A little interview. You know.

—Yeah.

—He was real enthusiastic. Really pumped. Said it was going to bring a ton of money into the county. Construction jobs for years.

—Yeah. His dad is on the county commission.

—That right? Young? Oh. Yeah. Buddy Young. That him?

—Yeah. Elected on a promise to bring jobs to the county.

—Hey. There's something new. A politician keeping his promise huh?

—Yeah. Funny how the son of the county commissioner suddenly shows up at the head of the development consortium.

I was being cynical. There was no reason to assume there'd been any back room dealing. But those damned county commissioners. Every one of them was all about growth growth growth. Bigger and better all the time. Shove another development down our throats. Raise taxes. Better schools. New pavement. New county office building. We can be the next Las Vegas. That fool Buddy Young would probably like it that way. Ruin the very thing that makes people want to live around here. The small town feel. Old Young. A great guy. Really. I voted against him. Not because I really care. About him I mean. I don't care whether he lives or dies. He can be king of the universe or run over by a cement mixer for all I care. But his whole campaign was about developing more stuff. Industrial parks. Homes. Schools. Holy shit. His opponent wasn't much better. Actually I knew nothing about that guy either—and cared less. But at least he mentioned the county budget in his campaign literature. As though it existed. As though the county actually had a budget. Maybe the guy didn't know much more than how it was spelled. B-U-D-G-E-T. But it was enough to earn my vote. Not that it mattered.

—But the thing they're really excited about is the fly-in-fly-out.

—What is that?

—Oh. I thought I'd mentioned it. The air strip.

—Air strip?

—Yeah. It is the centerpiece of the whole thing. Private airport. Private taxiways. Private hangars. You fly in from California. Taxi to your private hanger. Attached to your home. You know.

—Who can do that? Where are they going to find enough millionaire pilots to fill the stupid development?

—Oh. I don't know. That guy Young on the TV last night was saying that their California partners had a lot of interest. Claimed they were pre-selling lots.

—Yeah. I bet.

On the way home I stopped at the state liquor agency for a bottle of shiraz. I was alone. Normally we would commute together. But Michelle had used a sick day to take care of a couple of doctor's appointments. The liquor store was empty. Barb was sitting behind the counter. Fiddling with her phone. I came to the counter with two bottles. Michelle liked the sangria. It was on sale.

—Pretty quiet today?

—It is now. But we were hopping earlier.

—Yeah? Good business?

—I wouldn't say that. Not everybody was buying.

—Oh. Yeah.

—There is no bar in the neighborhood so people come in here to talk. I swear I'm like the local bartender. People want to come in and tell me all their problems.

—Yeah.

—And. Let me tell you. People got problems. Shew. You should hear some of the stories.

—Pretty bad huh?

—Yeah. And graphic. I mean there are just some things I don't need to know.

—I can understand.

—I should write a book. The things I could tell.

—A real page turner.

—Yeah. Except I'd probably get sued. Everybody in town would sue me.

—Better hire a lawyer before you start writing.

I was standing at the door. Barb stopped talking. Looked me in the eye. Smiled.

—Have a good evening.

—You too.

Michelle had dinner ready when I got home. I poured the wine. We sat and ate. We'd been married for five or six months. And sometimes I still couldn't believe it. Coming home to a house with her in it. Not empty. We'd sit at dinner for hours. We'd talk. About everything. But about books mostly. Stegner. Fitzgerald. Percy. Harper Lee. Camus. DeVoto. A.B. Guthrie, Jr. Ayn Rand. O'Connor. Sinclair Lewis. Dostoyevsky. McCarthy. Cather. Horgan. Parkman. Bancroft. Kierkegaard. Hemmingway. Especially Hemmingway.

—What's wrong?

—Oh. You know. I'm just a jerk.

—OK.

—I'm sure it's fine.

—What?

—The new development.

—Oh. The one out in the valley? Other side of the freeway?

—Yeah. I just heard about it.

—I'm sorry.

—I guess it has been in the news.

—A little. They are calling it Meadowlark Ranch.

I laughed. Mirthlessly. A croak.

—Meadowlark! The only thing about meadowlarks is that they are being displaced. The meadowlark is now a refugee.

—I know. It is bad.

—We're going to have to move.

—Move where?

—Yeah. There is nowhere to go. They are everywhere. The developers.

—I'm sorry.

Michelle. She was a gem. She really was. She listened to me. Let me vent. Let me shout. Let me cry and kick the furniture. And I did it too. I stood up and kicked a chair. Shouted. FUCK. Took a deep breath. Sat down again.

—I have a surprise for you.

—You do?

—Yeah.

—What?

—After dinner. We'll go see.

—What is it?

—When I was done at the doctor's office I went for a walk. You know that pink double wide on the next block?

—The one on the south side of the street with the front yard full of dog shit and the massive Dodge dually parked on the sidewalk?

—Yeah.

—What about it?

—It's for sale.

ABOUT THE AUTHOR

Walker Wallace is originally from Texas. He has lived and worked in Arizona, Nevada, and Utah. He currently lives in Santa Barbara, California. He enjoys walking on the beach with his two dogs.

www.ingramcontent.com/pod-product-compliance
Lightning Source LLC
Chambersburg PA
CBHW060422130626
46555CB00005B/2168

* 9 7 8 0 6 9 2 5 7 8 2 2 3 *